Acknowledgments

Some of these pieces have appeared previously in magazines, often in different forms. To the editors of these publications, all acknowledgments and thanks are due.

"The Heir," *The Massachusetts Review*
"Pain," *The Southern Review*
"Cuckold," "Embrace," "Abandoned," *Western Humanities Review*
"The Date," *Savvy*
"Biopsy," "The Wig," "Turquoise," *New Directions*
"Angry," *New York Woman*
"Transfigured Night," *Boston Globe* magazine
" 'Shot,' " *Seventeen*
"Letter, Lover," *Fiction*
"My Madman," *Exile*
"The Mother" and "From *The Life Of . . .*" *Shenandoah*
"Insomnia," *Onthebus*
"The Artist," *Omni*
"The Maker of Parables," *Kenyon Review*
"Where *Is* Here?" *American Short Fiction* (Number 1, Spring 1991, published by University of Texas Press)
"The Escape," *Triquarterly*
"Bare Legs," *Stand* (England), *Yale Review*
"Actress" and "Forgive Me!" *Michigan Quarterly Review*
"AREA MAN FOUND CRUCIFIED," *Southern California Anthology*
"The Ice Pick," *Raritan*
"Lethal," *Ontario Review*
"Imperial Presidency," *Boulevard*
"Running," *Self*
"Sweet!" *Antæus*
"Beauty Salon" *The Gettysburg Review*

Where *Is* Here?

Other Books by Joyce Carol Oates

Where *Is* Here?

STORIES BY

Joyce Carol Oates

THE ECCO PRESS

The Ecco Press
100 West Broad Street
Hopewell, NJ 08525
Published simultaneously in Canada by
Penguin Books Canada Ltd., Ontario
Printed in the United States of America
Designed by Debby Jay
First paperback printing, 1993

Library of Congress Cataloging-in-Publication Data

Oates, Joyce Carol, 1938–
Where is here?: stories / by Joyce Carol Oates.—1st ed.
p. cm.:
I. Title.
PS3565.A8W44   1992   813'.54—dc20   92-3634   CIP
ISBN 0-88001-283-8
ISBN 0-88001-338-9 (pbk.)

The text of this book is set in Trump Mediaeval.

For Emily Mann

Contents

In the end I would much rather be a Basel professor than God; but I have not dared push my private egoism so far as to desist for its sake from the creation of the world. You see, one must make sacrifices however and wherever one lives.

—Nietzsche, in a letter to Jacob Burckhardt,
6 January 1889

Where *Is* Here?

Lethal

I just want to touch you a little. That delicate blue vein at your temple, the soft down of your neck. I just want to caress you a little. I just want to kiss you a little—your lips, your throat, your breasts. I just want to embrace you a little. I just want to comfort you a little. I just want to hold you tight!—like this. I just want to measure your skeleton with my arms. These are strong healthy arms, aren't they. I just want to poke my tongue in your ear. Don't giggle! Don't squirm! This is serious! This is the real thing! I just want to suck a little. I just want to press into you a little. I just want to penetrate you a little. I just want to ejaculate into you a little. It won't hurt if you don't scream but you'll be hurt if you keep straining away like that, if you exaggerate. Thank you, I just want to squeeze you a little. I just want to feel my weight against your bones a little. I just want to bite a little. I just want a taste of it. Your saliva, your blood. Just a taste. A little. You've got plenty to spare. You're being selfish. You're being ridiculous. You're being cruel. You're being unfair. You're hysterical. You're hyperventilating. You're provoking me. You're laughing at me. You want to humiliate me. You want to make a fool of me. You want to gut me like a chicken. You want to castrate me. You want to make me fight for my life, is that it?

You want to make *me* fight for my life, is that it?

AREA MAN FOUND
CRUCIFIED

Discharged from U.S. Army "disability" pension and a loose flap
of skin over the hole they bored in my skull. Don't tell me they
didn't plant one of those silicon chips inside. The size of a louse.
I'm dead meat but not *that* dead. Sons of bitches, it's not just the
cruelty toward their fellow man (and I am a white man, a Cauca-
sian) but the failure to respect. That's what pisses us off. You're a
pvt. first class all your life. It's all rank. Wore a suit, a tie, dark socks
to explain my case at the VA. Bitch with a silver whistle the size
of a thimble around her neck she went out into the corridor to blow.
Didn't I hear it? Escaped down the fire escape, fell, broke my leg in
two places. The VA claimed no record of me! Would not pay.
Refused. My own father, in his underwear, was held up to public
ridicule. Also my mother, who was in the courtroom the time I had
a jury trial, her diabetes made her sleepy and when she nodded off
the judge yelled at the bailiff to clear that woman out of his court
like she was trash. It's been passed down in the family. Now I'm
an old bastard myself. I thrive on adversity. This preacher in the St.
Anthony's shelter trying to tell us what's God's love. Suffer little
children. That shit. So I hauled off and punched the asshole in the
gut. Tell me about love, asshole. I got no love to spare I said. Tell
that to the babies stuffed down the toilets! Later somebody said I

2

was speaking a language sounded like German. Some foreign language. I couldn't make any sense of it and naturally supposed it was erroneous, then afterward realized it was the silicon chip responsible. Still, the VA would not pay. I put my fingers plus thumbs in the flame on a gas stove at my sister's to alter the prints. It's what you are driven to in this nation. Served three months at Red Bank, for passing checks. Served fourteen months at Jackson, checks and "resisting arrest." Meaning a plainclothes cop mashes your face against a wall, bounces your head off a urinal never once explaining who he is, or why. Knees you in the kidneys so you're pissing blood for a week. The other time, I was staying at the Hotel Niagara, paying by the week, and they called the cops claiming the room was damaged, fist holes in the walls and the toilet crapped up. Again, escaped out rear window. Learned Momma had passed away, while I was in Red Bank. No word. Many a man will regret that omission. 1975–1988 many travels. You must keep in motion to block surveillance. They use a big dish satellite out of Washington, D.C. The FBI. Your travels and your thoughts are gauged, then it's on microfilm. You can thwart it if you know how. A woman promised she'd remove the chip in my brain with a tweezers. I believed her. I am a fool for pretty women, I don't care what color they are. Took all my cash and shoes. My Bible, with Momma's snapshot taken in her casket. Somebody said, that's disrespect, the snapshot of Momma was a double exposure with some girls on a beach in teeny-weeny bathing suits like they wear now, but that was an accident. Also, I didn't know those girls. I didn't touch a one of them no matter what they said. And I'm not going back to the hospital: try me. Hosed down the drain. Crucified. I climbed on the table in the cafeteria before any of the orderlies could stop me, I spoke of the capitalist system leeching a man white, then spitting him out like a rind. It causes the death of a noble woman like my Momma before her time. It causes a woman pure-hearted like my first wife to grab hold of a crying baby, our mutual son, and thump him on the floor so both his knees shatter. Crucify me, I was shouting. You done every other thing to me so crucify me, that's all that's left. Sixteen days in a straitjacket, isolation. Covered in my own shit. You think a man's going to forget? Discharged, went to

St. Paul staying with my sister. Came home one night, the fire
trucks were in the street, the cops. A claim of "suspected arson."
All my clothes, personal papers, ID, my Bible and precious possessions. No justice. The insurance company claimed "act of God."
My own sister betrayed me, a telephone call. Like Judas. She said,
Oh I do not want to do this, but— My first wife said those same
words, Oh I do not want to do this, but— Then they slide the
needle in. Then they slice you open like a fish, gut you clean.
Escaped to Gary, Indiana. Worked six weeks for U.S. Steel, melt
shop. The product was I-beams. Vision in right eye permanently
impaired. Lungs riddled with steel filings. The union busted me for
"false ID," called in actual cops in their hire. Beat me, left me for
dead. The man whose union card I had *was* me, but the VA claimed
otherwise. A married woman took me in. Angel of mercy, she was.
Met at the dog races where, it's strange, it's a fact of life, people are
undersize mostly—they are not big, or tall like me. She was married
but her husband was missing two years. "Suspect of foul play." It
was a mixed neighborhood. Things happened by broad day. Tampa,
Florida. Roaches big as your fist. Trailer park. Next door, guy had
a .45-caliber Commander. The FBI was on my trail picking up
signals I guess from the chip. I never touched that gun. No prints
of mine. Cops came to question me after the robbery but had to let
me go. I'm legally blind I said. I can't find my way to the fucking
toilet I said. Later I was in Houston, Texas. Saw this plaster-of-paris
Jesus Christ on a cross, fucker must have been twelve feet high.
Scared the shit out of me. His heart exposed, and His eyes. A year
later, in the St. Anthony's shelter for men, I was beaten mercilessly
for preaching the truth. I don't mean Jesus, I mean the rational
mind. I mean Jesus in his physical torment. They kicked me out of
the shelter for drunk-and-disorderly. Taking no mind for how I was
pissing blood. So I woke up under this bridge, and these kids came
along. These kids beating up on bums, especially white guys. Down
in Houston the kids'll snort anything—aerosol spray cans, paint
thinner. They'll do anything for a buck. I said, Here's all the cash
in my pocket plus my shoes, here's nails, a hammer, you know
what to do. There was an old billboard next to the bridge, sign for
Coors beer but it's all torn off, tattered. I said, Right there, see, my

feet can rest on that ledge. They were eyeing me like some old fart. Rail-tailed hair, eyes like somebody's thumb had been gouging them, mouths like dogs grinning. They were spics, and a nigger or two. Or all light-skinned niggers. You can't tell their ages—a ten-year-old's the size of his own daddy. Estrogen from red meat and eggs does it. They're all on welfare. Our tax money is fatting them up. Ashes to ashes, dust to dust, I said. They were wondering what to do then one of them yells, Gimme the beat! and the little fucks jump me laughing in my face, take my money and my shoes leave me bleeding on the ground. Came north, then. To St. Paul. Fortu- nately, the VA had me stamped *overseas dead* which is the deadest kind of dead meat. So no trace. Born here fifty-eight years ago but no trace. Arrested vagrancy, drunk-and-disorderly, stripped me naked and forced me into a gas shower. Claiming lice, but I know better. Authorities deny any such showers in the United States, but those who survive know a different story. Once, a mobile TV crew came along interviewing people for Fourth of July, what are your plans for Fourth of July they were asking, tried to avoid me but I stepped right up, I took the microphone out of this bleached- blonde's hand and started saying how I had been stripped naked and forced to endure a gas shower in that very city. It was a clear public protest but nothing came of it. Freedom of speech and of assembly in the United States gets you nowhere. A kick in the ass. But I was north now among friends. Even the niggers here talk better. Woke under this bridge where there's laughter echoing up under the gird- ers. And these kids come along. Five of them. I figure they're looking for me, and I'm sure looking for them. I'm a tough old bastard, I'm skinny but I'm tough. Born here fifty-eight years ago did I say that? I got these rusted twisty nails and a hammer and I'm pointing up to the railroad trestle where there's some T-beams like a cross. Here's my cash and my shoes I'm telling these kids. My signet ring. It's actual gold. It has an onyx, and gold. The kids are saying, Man, you're crazy. Cutting their eyes at one another, gig- gling. I smelled the beer they were belching. White kids, too. I said, I was talking kind of loud, I said, It's you or somebody else who comes along here next, you want my money or don't you? Standing there scuffing their feet. Little grins passing among them like minnows. They're hot to do it, but they're scared. Thinking, What the fuck is this old guy after? I started yelling at them. I swung the hammer in the air. Saying, My kidneys are leaking blood. In my left eye there's a blaze of light like a burning fuse. Jesus showed the way, He's the way, the truth, and the light. King of the assholes. Every human baby comes into the world thinks he's hot shit then one fine day wakes up to the fact he's shit. They're looking at me, and I'm looking at them. Watch out, man, they're saying. I'm saying, Look, my momma loved me just like every other momma loves her baby, or ought to. Hugged and kissed and one day I was crying hard like a baby will and she picked me up under the arms not knowing what she did (for so the woman will swear, and I am not one to doubt) and thumped me on the floor, hard. Both knees broken and never been the same since. Legs bowed like a chicken wishbone. The mayor of St. Paul singled me out of a crowd, a crippled kid riding his old man's shoulder all hot and excited in the face, it's V-J Day August '45 and the mayor is being driven through the streets of the poor in his fancy black limousine like a hearse, he sees me, grins and gives me the V-sign, that happy day never to come again to these United States. Okay, asshole, you think you are singled out for a special destiny but it comes to this: a rotting railroad trestle, rusty bent nails, a claw hammer out of somebody's pickup truck. Here's my money, you little fucks, I tell them. Get busy.

Imperial Presidency

For weeks our town prepared for his arrival, excitedly, but with apprehension—for what if something went wrong? Never in the history of our remote region had any President appeared in our midst, never had we been so honored, from Federalist times until now.

The President's schedule allowed him to visit us only briefly, from 10:50 A.M. to 11:30 A.M. of Saturday, May 18. He was to speak at the unveiling of a monument honoring area soldiers who had sacrificed their lives in our most recent war; the monument, commissioned by our Rotary Club and executed by a local sculptor, was a hefty, seven-foot cast-iron likeness of several soldiers, in the old-fashioned heroic mode—two white boys, a black, and another of ambiguous racial heritage, foot soldiers all. The monument was to replace a granite sculpture of a Civil War general on horseback, badly mottled by weather and pigeon droppings, in the concrete square in front of the county courthouse, adjoining our two-acre "green."

What industry, what communal activity, preparing for the President's visit! Facades of municipal buildings, filthy with the grime of decades, were sandblasted and hosed down. Crumbling masonry on the courthouse was repaired. Stores facing the square were spruced up, and untenanted buildings were refurbished by the township. On the south wall of the old armory, long a local eyesore, happy platoons of schoolchildren painted a mural in bright primary colors, trees, flowers, airplanes, blue sky, and fluffy white clouds.

On the concrete square in front of the courthouse, where the monument was placed and the ceremony was to be held, carpenters built a raised wooden platform large enough to hold twenty persons. An enormous flag was draped across the courthouse facade, and twenty-four small flags festooned the platform. Since the park was weedy in some spots and barren in others, as with the mange, squares of thick green turf had to be quickly laid in, at considerable expense. Park benches were repaired and repainted; those rotted or damaged beyond repair were replaced by benches borrowed from other township parks. Chainsaws buzzed and whined for days as crews of workers trimmed dead wood from trees or cut down trees altogether. Spring flowers—tulips, pansies, brilliantly colored aza-leas—were put in the long neglected beds bordering the square and in earthenware pots on the courthouse steps. The numerous derelicts and homeless folk who inhabited the park were banished under threat of being jailed, and the square was patrolled by mounted policemen.

How attractive the area was looking, at last! How proud we were!

A week before the President's arrival, Secret Service men came to town to confer with local authorities regarding security measures. There were rumors of protests, assassination threats—thus, the President would have to be protected at all times. Directives were issued ordering the "impacting" of all buildings bordering the square, from 9:00 P.M. of May 17 to the President's departure on the morning of May 18; parking was to be prohibited on most downtown streets on the morning of May 18, and, of course, the route the President's cavalcade would take to the square was to be cordoned off. Lists were made of all area residents who had ever drawn attention to themselves as critical of any government, whether federal, state, or local, or any elected or appointed public official, and given to the Secret Service for its own purpose.

For, how fearful we were, that in the midst of this historic event something disastrous would happen!

The morning of May 18 dawned chill, with a light, gritty drizzle borne by a northeast wind, bringing the odor of chemical factories upriver that we had so hoped—prayed!—would be blown in another direction. A pale glowering sun appeared grudgingly through scrims of cloud. How disappointed we were, yet how hopeful that, by the time of the President's arrival, the sky would clear!

Early, even before the crowd began to gather in the square and on adjoining sidewalks, security officers were in evidence—some in uniform and some plainclothes; there were mounted police, state troopers on motorcycles, Secret Service men in dark suits, with ties, stationed conspicuously in doorways and on top of roofs. With so much security, the mood of the crowd was subdued; little excitement was expressed until the President's helicopters were sighted—how loud their roaring!—their spinning propellers like crazed birds' wings!—and a muffled cheer went up. The helicopters landed, seemingly without incident, a mile north of the square; within minutes, the cavalcade of several bulletproof black limousines was making its way along the cordoned-off route. The President was here! At last, the President *was* here!

Everyone strained to see, to memorize. The President was helped out of his limousine and, accompanied by his aides, mounted the platform, where he was greeted, effusively, by our Mayor and other local officials. Applause continued, though a bit hesitantly. For *was* this the President, after all? We had seen the great man on television numberless times, and his likeness in newspapers and magazines, but we had never seen him in the flesh before and did not know quite what to think.

As the ceremony began, with our Mayor's welcoming speech and the dramatic unveiling of the monument—from which, a bit awkwardly, a sheet of semitransparent plastic was being drawn—we studied the President with fascination and curiosity, like small children, paying attention to little else. At first, so white and rubbery was his facial skin, we thought he was wearing a mask; then, seeing that his forehead gleamed oily with perspiration, and that his small close-set eyes darted about nervously, and his tiny pink rosebud mouth sucked inward, as if in thought, we concluded that this must be his face—his actual face. But how thin, how pale and haggard, he appeared! And how much older than his reputed age!

There had been rumors out of Washington of a mysterious illness, or a congeries of illnesses; and angry denials of such rumors, and proclamations of the President's health.

Yet it seemed quite clear to us, as the President took the podium, striding with an air of forced vigor, and swaying as he clutched the sides of the podium, that this was not a well man.

Several times, beginning his speech, he had to stop, to cough into a tissue, short, harsh, hacking coughs that brought up clots of phlegm; this tissue was then taken quickly from him by one of his aides and thrust into a paper bag. By this time, in answer to our heartfelt prayers, the drizzle had ceased; the wind had shifted out of the poisonous northeast; a pale glaring sunshine illuminated the platform of dignitaries and fluttering flags, as if a curtain were being drawn.

Exposed now by the direct sunshine, the President *did* look infirm, and bore little resemblance to the man of smiling vigor we knew from television and print. What we had concluded was the man's face was in fact a mask, an ingeniously lifelike rubber mask that fitted his skull tightly, covering every inch of facial skin, with obligatory holes, of course, for mouth, nostrils, and eyes; it covered some of his hair as well or, rather, his bald pate, for part of the President's head was hairless, and this part of the mask was rippled and painted dark brown, to suggest real hair, yet—and this is what I mean by ingenious!—what remained of the President's actual hair was somehow threaded through slits in the head covering, so that his own hair and the painted rubber hair melded together. Had it not been for the wind stirring this "real" hair, which had been dyed a dark brown to match the painted hair, the casual observer might have supposed that the President had no hair at all except painted rubber hair—which would have been grossly misleading.

The rubber mask left openings for the President's ears, which were unusually small, shallowly whorled ears, but it covered his neck and disappeared inside his stiff white shirt collar. It was creased and ridged as if with the burden of tragic thought and, as I'd indicated, covered with a thin gleaming film of perspiration, or oil of some kind, most noticeable on the man's forehead, where the thought creases were most prominent. When the President coughed, the corners of his little rubber mouth puckered, and, wiping irritably with a tissue, he had some difficulty clearing away the sputum from the mouth, so that, during his speech, saliva gleamed there distractingly, rust-flecked as if with blood.

As I'd also indicated, the President was much thinner and far more haggard than we expected. He had the dazed look of a man who has not dressed himself and cannot locate parts of his body. His necktie was tightly knotted against his rubber Adam's apple, his shirt cuffs had slipped down around his hands, as if the sleeves were too long for his arms. The shoulders of his gray pinstripe suit were prominently, boxily, padded, and his trousers were a size too large for his wasted frame; his fly zipper was partway undone but, fortunately, hidden from frontal view by the podium and the phalanx of fluttering flags. And his hands shook. Ah, it was distracting, how the President's hands, gripping his speech, shook, as if the very platform beneath him were violently vibrating!

The President read off his prepared speech in a high, quavering voice, pausing frequently as if confused by a word or a phrase he had never seen before, or did not comprehend, or, with desperate snuffling snorts, to clear his sinuses of phlegm. (Which, then, turning irritably aside, he would spit into a tissue; and hand the tissue to his embarrassed aide.) The speech began with gratitude for the "brave, fallen compatriots" who were being memorialized in "this major work of civic art" this morning; then it shifted to the "sacred" obligation of the President to maintain, if not to actively expand, our country's "imperial role" in the world; then, to the wickedness of plotting "politically motivated" adversaries in Congress who wished to challenge the President on these issues; then, in a rhapsodic conclusion evoking both Abraham Lincoln and Thomas Jefferson, the need to entrust the President with foreign policy in all particulars, above all the power of declaring war on our country's enemies. Some of the force of the conclusion was mitigated by a fresh attack of coughing.

The President then turned away, blinking in the pale sunshine, as if not knowing what to do next. Taking their cue, all the gentlemen on the platform leapt to their feet and began to applaud. So too the crowd applauded, in a wavering manner at first, then, as the President squinted out into the square, a small smile giving life to his rosebud rubber mouth, we applauded more enthusiastically, and some of us even cheered and whistled. (Yet with restraint: the presence of so many security officers was dampening.) The President thanked us, adding, ad lib, that this "was a day to treasure always," and applause swelled, with more cheers and whistles.

The President's aide stepped forward to assist him back to his seat. The President tugged at the neck of the rubber mask, which must have been uncomfortable, yet, now, he did look a bit more relaxed and quite buoyed up by our applause.

So, the ceremony ended; the dignitaries left the platform in an orderly procession, as the enormous flag behind them took the sunlight fully, all brilliant satiny red, blue, white; the crowd was urged to disperse quietly, not to linger.

Nothing disastrous had happened! At last, we had entered history. Shortly afterward workers quickly dismantled the platform; removed the flags; hauled away the tubs of flowers and certain of the park benches. With a powerful hose from the firehouse workers hosed down the square, where clots of blood-tinged sputum stained the concrete. Days, weeks, now months later, these stains are still to be seen, deep in the concrete, like ghost coins.

Bare Legs

The weather had turned, it was early October and the nights damp, cold, still the first glimpse he'd had of her, walking swiftly across the parking lot at Chet's Keyboard Lounge, was the pale flash of her bare legs. The thin, silky material of her skirt was blowing about her knees, she was staggering a little in the high-heeled shoes, but not drunk, no one had ever seen her drunk. Where she'd come from exactly he didn't want to wonder, that night—just saw, yes, she was alone, and in a hurry. Knowing her destination and what she wanted, or anyway giving that impression.

Her name was Rhonda. That was what it sounded like when she said it, quick and sort of flurried, a West Virginia twang. No last name and no telephone number, no address because she was "moving," she said, or "looking for a place," she said. None of that mattered, all that mattered—and now she'd be speaking fast, worried—was finding her kids that were lost: her daughter, Shannon, who was fourteen years old and her little boy, Peter. You seen these kids? You heard about these kids? She'd pass snapshots along the bar, maybe a dozen of them, back in the booths where she'd sit sometimes if she could tolerate sitting for more than a few minutes, she was high-strung, jumpy, you could feel the heat coming off her skin, and her eyes showing white above the iris, a good-looking woman but something a little wrong, that quick sharp giggle, the fleshy-shivery body, very "feminine."

13

That was a trademark of hers, the guys told him: Rhonda's a real lady, whatever else.

Help me find them, you guys, huh? Will you? She'd be smiling, squinting, passing the snapshots around, this was evidence, wasn't it, these were real kids she'd had and lost and she was determined to find them, she needed help that was all, any help, anybody? Her voice was low and throaty, and had that twang. Her face was small, with a short upper lip, pug nose, glossy lips, perfume. Lots of perfume. She wore tight-fitting bright-colored dresses, lime green, crimson, silky stuff summer knits, cheap clothes but attractive, never trousers, still less jeans, and never flat-heeled shoes. Hey— you gonna help me? Please?

In one of the snapshots Shannon was maybe six years old, in another she was suddenly ten, in another a teenaged girl, pouty lipsticked lips and pinched little triangular face with that pug nose like Rhonda's. It was Peter that really got to your heart—this sort of goofy-sweet kid, little guy about seven in most of the snapshots, blond, hair in tufts, eyes set close together and shining like glass marbles in the camera's flash. In one snapshot Peter was in paja-mas, in another in a bathtub looking up grinning. The first night he met her he'd asked was she divorced? had her husband gotten custody? were the kids runaways? what about the police, had she contacted the police? and she started talking fast and sort of wild, shaking her head, she wouldn't trust the police with her own self, she said, let alone her children, they're agents of Satan, everybody knows. That hillbilly twang like a razor blade's edge.

Then she'd start crying, quick and angry as a child, run off to the ladies' room, repair the damage and return, but only to gather up the snapshots and take them to another booth or table or elsewhere along the bar. Help me find these kids, if you have any decency in your hearts, help me? I can't pay you right now, but I'll be in your debt forever. Hey, anybody seen these kids?

The snapshots were dog-eared, much creased, passed from hand to hand, even the guys who'd seen them before made a show of looking again, they were good guys mainly, but what could you do? Rhonda saying she had no last name, no telephone number, she was going to pass around like a whore—which was her word, ''whore,'' in that nasal angry-sounding West Virginia accent—she *was* a lady, sipped white wine slowly and elegantly holding the stemmed glass, never gin, whiskey, rarely beer, and never smoked, smoking was not only a sure sign of lowlife women, but real bad for your health as anybody in his right mind knows.

What freaked her out was if a snapshot was missing. Or she thought one was missing. Dropped underfoot, mislaid, she'd accuse one of the guys of being in the league of Satan, crying, hysterical, Where is it? who's got it? why are you tormenting me? Sometimes she'd talk of Satan as if he were outside in the parking lot, waiting. Her ex-husband was an old platoon buddy of Satan's, she'd say, laughing—taught each other all their tricks. The guys would laugh like it was a joke, which probably it was.

At Chet's Keyboard Lounge, at the Cloverleaf, at Hal's off the Turnpike, at Conte's at the Edison exit . . . it was at Conte's he happened to be sitting smoking a cigarette in the cab of his truck, motor running, just past Thanksgiving, and there she was suddenly out of nowhere, the woman who called herself Rhonda, sure it was her walking fast through the parking lot, the neon-winking puddled parking lot, and where'd she come from?—a trashy vacant lot on the other side of Conte's and the Turnpike beyond, and it looked like she was in a hurry, vehement in her stride, gripping her purse and bare-headed in a fake fur jacket, in those high-heeled shoes that must have hurt her feet like hell, bare feet bare heels bare legs in the cold rain, he was staring at her thinking it just blows you away sometimes, when you aren't ready for it, like the earth splits open with some secret you can't name.

He'd forgotten the kids' names, but he remembered their faces, it all came back blowing him away, Christ, he opened the door and called to her, Rhonda! hey! and she stopped dead, and squinted over at him, smiling then like she knew him, though maybe not his name, climbing up into the cab breathless and laughing knowing she had a place for the night if she wanted it, and looking good: so feminine. Somehow she always managed to stay feminine, not hardened, kept her hair clean and combed and her clothes not too rumpled, the cheap shoes too a little scuffed and mud-splattered, but looking all right, glamorous, like she cared. Sure she cared. You wouldn't know right away there was much wrong with her except for her bare legs in winter, the cold goose-pimply feel of them, the short sharp stubble pushing through where she hadn't shaved in a long while.

Turquoise

The name everyone knew is Sherrill but the mother says that was never the name they gave her, the name on the baptism certificate is Lucille Ann.

Wild curly red hair, couldn't get a comb through it. Big shoulders, thighs. Sitting at the back of the room in high school yawning into a compact mirror, licking her lips, rubbing her tongue over her front teeth. Tight black orlon sweater, shiny black belt cinched in tight, that lacy white blouse from Grant's the boys went crazy over, brassiere straps, even the cups of the brassiere, heavy lazy breasts. One of her boyfriends gave her a turquoise stone on a skinny gold chain so she wore it most days. It's real turquoise, she told the other girls.

She quit school and went to live with a man on the Yewville Pike, twenty years older, his wife had gone off and left him with two small children. Sherrill said she hadn't had anything to do with the wife going off but nobody believed her. Then she lived with a man named Verrill or Vurill, then she messed around with other guys, some married some not, she had so many boyfriends, the sheriff says, makes it harder than hell to figure out who did it.

Six months pregnant, playing pool at the Millside Inn, Saturday nights. Came with one boyfriend, might leave with another. Daddy goes to another tavern so there's no chance of them running into each other. She plays Elvis on the jukebox. Sings "Don't Be Cruel,"

"Heartbreak Hotel," which were old before she was born. Sometimes a boyfriend will meet up with a brother but the brothers are
cool, got enough problems of their own. It's the mother: going
around whining, saying slut, bitch, broke my heart, tramp, owes me
money, she don't dare show her face out at the house.

There are two sisters remaining in the family, five brothers, and
the mother—"next of kin," "survivors"—the story on the front
page of the weekly paper is only a few inches long. Snapshot from
high school, Sherrill with a big smile, big front teeth, eyebrows
drawn on like crayon, separate lashes stiff with mascara. She is
wearing a string of pearls around her neck. Prim little puff-sleeved
sweater.

She disappears over a Labor Day weekend, she's missing for a
month, then some boys fishing in the canal happen to discover part
of an arm sticking up through the mud. Murderer was too damn
lazy, the sheriff says, to dig down more than a foot. Water and muck
keep filling in. The men start their careful digging, one of the
deputies takes photographs stage by stage. An arm with no hand, a
head with eyes gone and part of the jaw missing, hair stuck in the
mud, what looks like a necklace grown into the chest. Water, muck,
mud, hair, decomposing flesh and the fabric of her slacks and shirt
all grown together. The sheriff's men work slowly. Unearthing
treasure, it looks like. None of the onlookers, even the youngest
boys, says much, getting their feet wet in the marshy soil, a light
gray drizzling rain. The men have all afternoon to do the job right,
the light won't start fading until after six.

Biopsy

In her girlhood of some years ago she'd been a serious swimmer, so all this constituted really was swimming in uncharted unrefereed waters, the space of time she would have to endure between what her doctor took pains to call the "surgical procedure" (*not* an "operation") on Tuesday morning and the ringing of her telephone Thursday morning, 8:30 A.M. approximately, when his office would receive the laboratory test results from Philadelphia. So it wasn't infinity but merely forty-eight hours more or less of which she might spend as many as fourteen hours unconscious, two nights of seven hours' sleep each (if not natural sleep then drugged sleep—she would be taking a morphine derivative for the pain), which left thirty-four hours of consciousness of which she could count on as many as ten hours spent in the preparation and consumption of meals and the kitchen cleanup afterward if she stretched things (why not telephone people as soon as she got home, invite them for an impromptu party tomorrow evening, spend much of the afternoon tomorrow preparing an ambitious meal, then the evening would be entirely taken up in eating, drinking, sociability, no one would guess the state of her nerves and their not knowing might cancel out that state—swimming isn't always against the current after all), which left twenty-four hours, a nightmare of time if you stared unblinkingly into it, but she had her work, and she had the tasks of her household, and she had reading, and she had the tele-

phone—she might call, for instance, her mother (with whom since
her father's death she was close, yet distant—close in her feeling for
her, distant in her guardedness about revealing much of herself
to her), and there were friends, of course, and former lovers if it
came to that, that degree of desperation, but she was resolved that
it would not. For there was, again, her work, her work that *was* her
in the deepest and most abiding sense, and even if in the middle of
the night she found herself incapable of sleep she could force herself
to work—had she not done so upon other difficult occasions? And
should that strategy fail she would leave the house like stepping
boldly out of her skull and walk (she was walking now, in fact) and
walk and walk until her lean muscles ached with a pleasant tired-
ness and her body was bathed in a dreamy haze of perspiration and
sleep would have become unnecessary.

Say she has gotten through the nights. Say she has gotten through
forty-seven and one-half hours. Thursday morning and she has been
awake since dawn, showering calmly and grooming herself in that
matter-of-fact way she has cultivated over twenty-odd years to ac-
commodate, not loneliness, but aloneness, the primary fact of her
life, and now she is staring out the window, warming her hands
around a mug of hot tea, reasoning that it is only a matter of
duration now, a final effort, the shore at last visible beyond the
choppy waves, and the land beyond it, so rich, suddenly, with
possibility—how like tracery it is, that shore she has never glimpsed
before, that land, that horizon, as if an idea only, her idea, waiting
to be filled in.

The Date

Two city buses, Friday rush hour, so I was late getting downtown: had a date to meet this man at 6 P.M. in the bar of the Brass Rail and it was five minutes to six and I hadn't changed my clothes yet or made up my face, I could feel the desperation starting in my bowels.

Those days, I hadn't any money but I had hopes. High hopes, my mother spoke of them, not jeering but with affection. My eyes were clear most of the time, my natural instinct was to smile. In a gathering of my peers my face stood out intelligent and illuminated, if it was made up. You could say I was ambitious.

Four mornings a week I took classes at the downtown branch of the state university. Worked five afternoons a week, to pay tuition, and room and board at home, in the university hospital cafeteria. In my grease-splattered white nylon uniform, hair in an old-fashioned hairnet, flat-heeled shoes and white knee socks, and a face shiny as if scrubbed with steel wool, I wasn't fit to be seen by any man about whom I had hopes.

I had a tendency to fall in love in sudden angry spurts. Men flattered me, saying I resembled Jane Russell, in the face—the same dark eyes, bone structure. But only when my coloring was good and my thick dark brown hair was well brushed and I was wearing decent clothes.

That Friday, I was carrying a good jersey dress and high-heeled shoes in a shopping bag, my plan was to change somewhere close

21

by the restaurant but not *in* the restaurant because what if the man I was supposed to meet was already there? What if he happened to see me, looking pale and pinch-faced and plain like I did? before I was ready to be seen?

I'd only met this man the week before, Saturday night, with friends. His first name was Trevor, I didn't know his last name, and I couldn't predict any behavior of his.

I reasoned that I would have to change my clothes in the women's restroom of the Trailways bus station, so I'd have only half a block to walk, through an alley, to the Brass Rail. My new shoes were spike-heeled, shiny patent leather with open toes and thin straps I'd paid more for than I could afford, glamorous shoes but not very practical for walking, still less walking quickly along icy sidewalks. *Dear God*, I was whispering to myself, *help me: help me not to be late.*

When I got to the Trailways station it was already four minutes after six. The sensation deep in my bowels was stronger, like something churning, and I had to walk almost doubled over.

The women's room in the Trailways station was a familiar, dreary place: the kind of public place you never think of when you're away from it, but once you push open the door, step inside, you realize it has been there all along, waiting for you. The lipstick scrawls on the cinderblock walls, the mirrors specked with grime, stained sinks with hairs visible in the drains, stained toilets. I rushed in, steeling myself for some disagreeable sight or odor, and one of the mirrors showed me wild-looking in the face, damp eyes and a mouth that appeared lipless. I winced, looked away, refused to acknowledge myself before I was ready to be seen.

But I didn't have the restroom to myself as I'd hoped: a mother and a child were squeezed together in one of the toilet stalls. They were bickering, fussing, scolding. I would have waited until they left, but I was already late, and maybe someone else would come in anyway, so I went into one of the stalls farthest from theirs and fastened the latch and began to change my clothes. It was cramped in there, and clumsy, and my hands were shaking. I thought, *Dear God, dear God.* Such words running through my head were half pleas and half angry commands.

All week I'd been thinking of tonight. My date at the Brass Rail. I'd mentioned it casually to my mother, to a few friends. He had very black hair oiled and combed back from his forehead, I seemed to remember a fawn-colored suede jacket, a skidding-sly sort of smile like Richard Widmark's. He'd asked me my name and I told him and he said, My name is Trevor, and he'd smiled that smile and I'd felt the kick of it in my chest. We talked a while. I don't remember a word we said. It was banter, easygoing and friendly. Then he had to leave. Said he had another date, he had to leave. Damn it, had to leave. Only 11 P.M. and he had to leave, but maybe if I was free next Friday? we could meet downtown? at the Brass Rail, maybe? And I said Yes, maybe. Knowing I looked good, I could afford to play it cool, composed. My shoulder-length hair all beautiful waves brushed till it crackled with static electricity.

Tonight I wasn't the same person, it seemed, or I wasn't the same person yet, struggling to pull my uniform off over my head, banging my elbows against the sides of the toilet stall. The restroom was virtually unheated, but I'd begun to sweat, I could hear myself panting like a dog. I had a hard time getting the jersey dress down over my head and then I had to take off my knee socks and put on nylon stockings, charcoal-tinted stockings, I was in terror of getting a run in the stockings because I hadn't an extra pair and I hated to step onto the dirty tile floor, it *was* dirty, no telling what those stains were. Once or twice I felt lightheaded and had to lean against the wall, my watch wasn't reliable but I knew I was late and getting later by the minute and the queasiness in my bowels was an intensification of the queasiness in my bowels I felt all the time in those days, those years, it had a tendency to spark a headache right behind my eyes, and if the headache began my eyes would run with tears and I'd blink at the world through a haze of pain, half-blind but needing to pretend that I could see, that *nothing at all was wrong*.

The fearfulness of such states lay not in themselves, for I was accustomed to them at the age of twenty, but to the insights into which they released me, like a powerful beacon shining into a muddled dark: why are you here? what are you doing? What hope is there in this? how can you have so little shame?

At other times, I never thought of such things. You could say I was a born optimist.

The mother and her daughter were at one of the sinks now, still bickering, a faucet turned on hard. I peeked out through a crack and saw that the mother was white-haired, in her sixties, and that the daughter was no child but a woman of about thirty-five: retarded, with lank greasy hair, a meat-pie sort of face, lusterless eyes, and a high whining childish voice. So that was it! I thought. But before I had time to feel sympathy, or pity, or superiority, the daughter giggled as her mother helped her dry her hands with a big wad of paper towels, she said, "I love you, Mama," the word drawn out so it was *Maaaa-maaaa*, a perfect spondee. The mother said, "I love you, too, honey." Then they went out, leaving me alone in that place, heart beating hard and trembling fingers and the pain behind my eyes like smashed glass.

I had the shoes on by now, I'd buckled the tiny straps snug around my ankles, teetering on the spike heels I stepped out of the stall so I could finish buttoning up the dress without banging my elbows. My eyes were greedy and hopeful seeing the reflection in the mirror, not the face which wasn't ready yet to be seen but the dress, the good maroon jersey dress that showed my figure to advantage, breasts and cinched-in waist and slender graceful hips.

By my watch it was almost fifteen minutes after six, but I tried to maintain my composure, I reasoned that the man would not leave if he'd ordered a drink and surely he'd ordered a drink, I soaked paper towels in cold water and dabbed gently at my face not wanting to roughen it more than it was then I rubbed in moisturizer cream, then makeup out of a tube, a tanned fleshy shade with a fragrant scent, then I powdered my face with loose powder over the makeup so my skin gleamed smooth-looking and young and after all it *was* young—I wouldn't be twenty-one until next March, it was only November now.

Next, my eyes. My hand shook but I needed to do my eyes carefully as I could. Leaning over the sink, my face an inch or so from the mirror. I could see faint swipes of lipstick on the mirror from other girls leaning close, like this, breathing onto the glass.

Then my mouth. Glossy crimson lipstick. Blotted and redone and blotted again. Lips luscious as Jane Russell's.

Then my hair. I knew it smelled of grease from the kitchen but there was nothing I could do about that. Brush, brush, brush until it shone and crackled, I'd shampooed it that morning at home, gorgeous hair I'd been told all my life, there was nothing else I could do.

My uniform, my other pair of shoes, I'd jammed in the shopping bag. I'd have to lug them along on the date but maybe Trevor wouldn't notice.

It was difficult walking up the alley to the Brass Rail in the patent-leather shoes but I got there at last, twenty-five minutes after six, out of breath, panting, my vision blurred over with pain but I could handle that, I knew to enter the crowded barroom as if I was on camera, play it like someone who's accustomed to being late and to being waited for. At first I couldn't make out any faces, *Where is he? is he here?* I kept my nervous hands away from my face and hair blinking to get my vision clearer and after a moment I saw him, I believed it must be him, thinner than I recalled, his eyes recessed and cheeks hollow, Trevor, my date, raising a slow hand to signal me from the farthest end of the bar, looking me over, smiling, teeth like a skull's, liking what he saw, maybe.

Angry

The first time he saw E. she was angry: speaking quietly but passionately with a man, a stranger to him, though of about his age and height, and it was summer, and warm, and windy off the lake, and E. wore a white cotton dress cut to show her bare shoulders, her lovely tanned arms and shoulders, and there was her dark hair like a hazy cloud about her head and the tears shining in her eyes and in this quarrel she held herself composed, even dignified, and he was thinking, *How beautiful*, the bright chiaroscuro of the woman's dark-tanned skin and the glaring white of her dress, *How beautiful*. Never had any woman spoken in such a way to him in public or in private, nor had he ever known a woman of such eerie composure in the height of an emotion and the memory of her remained with him for days as vivid as any dream and he found he was looking for her everywhere and then as such things happen when he'd virtually given up there she was, so unexpectedly, in the IGA store where on Friday evenings, back late from New York City, he shopped swiftly and pragmatically for the weekend, there suddenly she was ahead of him in the check-out line in a summer knit sweater, a plain skirt, sandals, and this time too she was angry, both amused and angry since the cashier had struck not one wrong key but two wrong keys so E. was insisting upon a complete recounting of all her purchases which seemed to him only reasonable. He'd murmured, ''Good for you!'' but so quietly she didn't seem to hear.

He had made up his mind then to meet her, to know her, since he was already in love with her; and the first time they were together—meeting at the home of mutual friends, the following weekend—he told her some of this, not all, but some, and E. regarded him with mildly quizzical eyes, and he had a glimpse of himself through those eyes, the romance of his words, the oddness of them, and he laughed, liking it, himself and her.

Then they were lovers, finally. Finally in love; or near love. Then one would advance a little too precipitously and the other would instinctively withdraw, and when the first one, relenting, would return, the other would have soberly reconsidered; and this was love. And he looked at E. who was no less beautiful than she had ever been, and he was disappointed, not resentful but disappointed, for something was missing: what? E. was an emotional woman, but it was primarily happiness he saw in her, ease, laughter, occasional exasperation, but she was tactful in ways no other lover had known to be tactful, above all E. avoided quarreling with him. "I—no, never mind," she would say, and he would say, "What? What is it?" and she would shake her head, not answering, and he would persist, "What were you going to say? Please—" until finally after perhaps a year—they were living together now, they'd been talking of marrying—E. did speak to him sharply, and he saw that look in her face, and his heart pulsed as if she'd reached into him and touched it with her very fingers: and not in love.

So suddenly they were talking. Quietly, yet in anger. And then they were quarreling. Not so quietly. In anger. Yes, it was a true quarrel such as he'd never had, not quite like this. E.'s eyes were bright with tears, the pupils dilated. Her nostrils were dead white. She began to scream at him, at the persistence of him, his low-level goading voice, his puzzlement, his hurt, she screamed and accused him of—and he called her—he of all men! he! normally so softspoken and guarded!—and unthinking as a child she slapped him in the face, she was sobbing, the flat of her hand and the very center of his undefended face, his nose, his glasses that went flying; and not knowing what he did he'd grabbed the woman's shoulder and closed his fist—he, of all men!—striking the woman a blow thrown with his fullest strength, a strength he hadn't known he possessed,

yes, in that instant he meant to smash her face that was so beautiful, he felt the cartilage of the beautiful nose shatter, though
afterward begging her to forgive him, to marry him, he would say
he was sorry he was sorry sorry sorry: my God, how sorry.

The Ice Pick

There had been no weather for weeks, no distinguishing clouds from sky, warm rain from warm ashes. A man at this time much younger than his twelve grandchildren would ever remember him, yet, still, in middle age, older than he had ever believed he would be, began to harbor cruel and exciting suspicions of his wife.

The wife, the wife! Poor Grandma! Where *was* she if not in the kitchen rolling out yards of pale noodle dough, or pushing the carpet sweeper back and forth over the threadbare parlor floor, or, out back, hanging laundry on the sagging clothesline amid the creaking of rusted pulleys? The wife had never learned to read English because by the time she'd emigrated to America she was seventeen years old and already married. Instead, she said the rosary.

The husband had too much pride to question the wife directly, for that was not his way. And, on the face of it, he would have had to laugh derisively—*his* wife, seeing a lover on the sly? The wife was in her midfifties, with a plump, raddled, coarse-skinned face, small warm mud brown eyes beneath thick eyebrows; her cheeks were perpetually ruddy, as if with heat; in the lifetime since she'd been a bride in Budapest she had gained forty pounds, ten pounds for each baby. Broad flaring hips like sails, a thick waist, a doughy shelf of bosom. Stiff-laced corsets kept her ample flesh upright and firm, and, on the clothesline, hung like boards, too heavy to be stirred by the fiercest winds. Imagine, *her!*—the wife!—a secret appetite for betrayal, a lascivious flame, in *her!*

The husband pulled and gnawed at his mustache, grinning to himself. Well, anything was possible, in America!

He could read English, he was certain. It was speaking that gave him trouble. One day, someone who laughed at his speech might be stabbed to the heart—a notion that gave some small solace.

Yet the husband would never have guessed that the wife had a secret life except, one day, having had a quarrel with his foreman at the foundry, he left work an hour early. And, on the streetcar, approaching home, hanging from a sweaty strap as from a noose, the husband saw, on the street, the wife, *his* wife, in a dress like a yellow tulip and high-heeled shoes, tall, large-boned, shapely, her head high and her massive bun of silvery sand-colored hair shining, striding along the sidewalk! So swiftly, so determinedly! So *eagerly!*

The husband stared, craning his neck. Fellow passengers in the crowded car observed him bemused. A funny little man! That thick bristling graying-black Magyar mustache, enraged holes for nostrils. His eyes were dark and bulging. The cuffs of his long flannel underwear showed gray at his wrists, and a smell of tobacco, whiskey, and harsh antiseptic soap lifted from him. He carried his head hunched down, like a bull.

The wife, the wife! *His* wife! Where had she gotten that yellow dress?

Out of six painful pregnancies, four children. They had all grown up hurriedly and hurriedly moved away. The great American continent had swallowed them up like sand dumped in sand, which is hard to forgive.

The husband was too taken by surprise to push his way off the streetcar and run in pursuit. He gripped the strap, paralyzed. He told himself that the wife was shopping—of course. She was the wife, the wife did the shopping. That was what she did, was supposed to do, every day except Sunday. The Italian grocery, the butcher's, the five-and-dime. The husband told himself that the wife might have gone to midday mass or to visit a sick friend—there were so many sick wives and mothers in the neighborhood! So she had dressed up and worn shoes of the kind she hated because her bunions pained her so badly. Was that the explanation?

The husband had not liked to see the energy and buoyancy in the wife's stride, out there amid strangers. Had she ever walked in *his* direction like that? At their wedding, in a Budapest church, urged along on the arm of her father, the wife had crept forward so shyly, with such mincing steps, it almost seemed the aisle floor had tilted away and, in her billowing white wedding finery, the bride was moving backward!

Another upset awaited the husband when he hurried up the four floors to his apartment—empty rooms! This was disorienting. This was not right. So the wife *was* gone. Derisive silence greeted the husband as, blood pounding in his face, he rushed from room to room.

In the discolored bureau mirror, his reflection did not show until, in a fury, he rapped his knuckles against it.

An hour later, when the wife returned, laden with shopping bags, breathless and perspiring from the stairs, she gave a cry at seeing the husband home at such a time. Oh Jesus, Mary, Joseph!—was he fired from this new job?—so soon? The husband, red-eyed, saw to his bewilderment that the wife had managed somehow to change her clothes—she was wearing a shapeless cotton housedress, flesh-colored support hose, chunky black shoes like a man's. Her hair in its familiar bun had come loose and horseshoe-shaped wire hairpins stuck out about her head like question marks.

The husband said, sullenly, *Who* are you to ask *me?*

But he made up his mind to forget, for maybe he'd been wrong, and *would* have forgotten, except, a few days later—the same thing!

Again, the husband was returning to the neighborhood early, an hour and forty minutes early, having suddenly, in one of his abrupt moods, decided to walk off the job, and again he was on the streetcar, crouched and peering out the window, when, suddenly, his eyes took in the very sight he dreaded—the woman who was his wife, *his* wife! striding up the Erie Avenue hill, this time dressed in black. Her hair was coiled at the back of her head like a great lustrous doughnut and, on even this weatherless day, scintillated with light. How was it possible! How did she dare! The bitch! Passengers on the streetcar, seeing a short, square, bull-chested man with wild eyes and hair, gave him a wide berth.

By exerting his will like a black chuffing bellows the husband forced the streetcar to a halt in the middle of traffic and pushed and elbowed his way out.

Head lowered, he hurried in pursuit of the wife. At once he was perspiring, red in the face. Pigeons flew up before him and circled overhead with derisive coos. A plump baby, held by its young mother at an open window, laughed and pointed at him.

The bitch! The whore! Where was she going! The husband hurried, yet could not seem to catch up with the wife. How was she able to walk so quickly, she who, in even her orthopedic shoes, found walking a chore? And uphill, like a young girl going to meet her lover! The wife was wearing a handsome black dress of raw silk, last worn, the husband believed, at a funeral a decade ago and, surely, too tight for her now? Yet she was wearing it—a black, slinky fabric, as in what was called lingerie, displayed in one of the big downtown department stores. Bitch! *She* was on display!

There was no radiance on this muffled gray day except what played about the wife's densely coiled fair hair.

Along Erie—across Sixth—then to Lackawanna: where, out of a florist's doorway, a man, a stranger, tall, lithe, stepped out to walk beside the wife, as if by chance. The man was holding a single long-stemmed rose which, glancing slyly at the wife, he touched to his nose—and then to hers. How was it possible!

The husband stared, astonished. He had suspected but—could he believe? Even, seeing, *believe?*

Oblivious of their surroundings, the wife and the stranger walked on, casting sidelong looks at each other, wetting their lips with their tongues. The husband, far behind now, unable to keep pace, could yet see—ah, he could not *not* see! The wife and her lover, *his* wife, smiling slyly, as if by accident allowing their hips to nudge each other. Where were they going? Would no one stop them?

A traffic light turned red and would not change. Endless streams of traffic passed in both directions. The husband saw, in the distance, the wife's lover take her hand and pull her off into a park, a greeny oasis of which the husband had had no prior knowledge, for rarely did he venture out of his neighborhood or take other routes to and from the foundry, and, squinting in disbelief, eyes nearly shut, he saw the lover roughly seize the wife in his arms—saw the wife laughingly slide her arms around her lover's neck as, with great appetite, and not the least sign of shame, they kissed—the red rose now held in the wife's fingers, bobbing aloft, like a speck of blood in the husband's very eye.

So, now, he knew.

Yet *what* did he know? For, late that afternoon, as the gray day slid to dusk, and the wife returned tired and ill-tempered to the apartment, it was much as before: the deception.

The wife was astonished to see the husband home again, early, and, moreover, sitting dazed and sullen at the kitchen table, drinking cheap whiskey. What, was he crazy?—drunk, and crazy? The husband was in his undershirt, and barefoot. His eyes were bloodshot. He gave off the foundry stink, unwashed. The wife let fall her heavy shopping bags onto a counter and snatched up her rolling pin, to protect herself, if needed; for often, at such times, protection *was* needed. But the husband raised his reddened eyes to the wife, in silence. They were tearful eyes! He saw that the wife had again changed her clothes, was again wearing one of her housedresses, stained and wrinkled. Her hair was dull as tarnished pewter. Gossamer-sheer stockings were gone, in their place the coarse cotton hose. A flaring-up of emotion gave life to the wife's sallow face, but the eyes were small and close set, the cheeks mottled as by a rash. How cunning the woman was, how cunning all women! It was something the husband had always suspected but only now *knew*.

The husband astonished the wife yet further by making no move to take the rolling pin from her, nor even to lurch to his feet in a rage.

Instead, he began to cry.

Later, in secret, the husband searched the wife's purse—finding nothing.

Yet later, in secret, while the wife was at mass, he searched through her bureau drawer, her intimate things—to discover, hidden beneath the wife's enormous billowing bloomers and canvaslike undergarments, a crushed rose.

It was ancient, virtually mummified. Giving off no smell. His hand trembled with the impulse to crush it further; but, instead, with a cunning of his own, he returned it to its hiding place.

So, now, he *did* know.

The following day, the husband did not go to the foundry at all. Instead he hid in the dank foyer of the building, beneath the stairs. When, in late morning, the wife left, he slipped out behind her to follow at a careful distance. He noted with disgust that, to disguise her intentions, she was wearing one of her old dresses. Her hips shifted as she walked, in hefty chunks, held in restraint by the corset beneath her clothes; the calves of her sturdy legs bulged like a man's. Her hair, pebble-colored, had been hastily wound into a knot at the nape of her neck.

Yet another day of no weather! The husband fingered the ice pick secret in the pocket of his denim work jacket.

This was the old ice pick, not the new. A bit rusted, thus less sharp. But sharp enough for its purpose.

Shrewdly, in English, the husband reasoned: no ice pick in the apartment, they would suspect *him.* For you would always have one ice pick, if you have an icebox. Yes? Isn't it?

The wife was making the rounds of the neighborhood stores, where she knew everyone, and everyone knew her. So much talk! chatter! gossip! with the other neighborhood wives. So this was the woman's pretense of a virtuous life.

The husband followed slyly, as he supposed. He did not seem to recognize people who spoke to him—if he did not see them, perhaps they did not see him. If he bumped into someone he muttered a growl that might have been anger, or apology. His mustache quivered. His dark eyes shone.

Why did the wife linger so, in the grocery? Fussing over the fresh produce, sniffing and exclaiming to herself. The big-bellied Italian grocer eyed her frankly and familiarly, his gaze taking in the wife's sturdy hips, heavy bosom, strong-boned jaws. And how slowly, sensuously, the wife drew her fingers over the damp green lettuce. . . . At the cash register, the wife laughed and blushed as the grocer muttered in her ear, God knows what lascivious remarks. The husband, watching from a shadowy corner of the store, felt his very soul abraded as with steel wool. That shrill girlish laughter! *He* had not heard it in thirty years.

Next, the husband followed the wife to the cobbler's—a dingy shop down an alley. Where, with a pretense of wifely solicitude and innocence, she dared bring one of *his* work boots to have its heel replaced. How buoyant the wife's step as she pushed through the door, how ruddy her cheeks, how hopeful her smile!—and how the hump-backed little cobbler, squinting up from his work, grinned at the sight of her! No mistaking it, they were old, intimate friends.

The cobbler, too? That misshapen little man?

It could not be possible!

For long terrible minutes the husband crouched in the alley, trying to look through the grimy window. He saw only shadows inside, heard only a murmur of voices, punctuated by laughter.

Shame suffused his being like a blood mist. He understood that everyone in the neighborhood must know of his wife's lovers and must be mocking him. Did even his grown children know? Could such a horror be?

At the butcher's, the husband could bear it no longer. By this time he was trailing the wife carelessly—others had begun to notice, and to stare after him, though the wife, intent upon her errands, did not. The husband watched as she entered the butcher's shop—stepping with seeming eagerness into that dreadful cave of raw carcasses, headless fowl, bloody innards, coils of fatty sausage, calves' brains, the rich heavy odors of blood and sawdust and animal terror. Here too the wife's shapely hips and bosom found approval in the butcher's eyes, the butcher was a white-haired youngish German with a way about him attractive to the ladies, who knows why?—and for long teasing minutes the two haggled together, ostensibly over the quality of a cut of pork loin, the price of beef liver. The husband gritted his teeth seeing through near shut eyes how the wife and the butcher dared poke their fingers together in the coarsest love play, squeezing and jabbing a quivering slab of liver!—with other customers, other wives of the neighborhood, close by!—and then he was rushing forward, and, amid screams of terror and disbelief, he was stabbing, stabbing, stabbing with the ice pick, a dozen, a hundred, a thousand times with the icepick, the wife's body, the butcher's body, her, him, again, again!—until their commingled blood flew everywhere, and their heavy bodies fell, like clothed carcasses falling, and the sawdust soaked up the rivulets of blood, and the husband was still screaming as strangers came to grip him from behind and to wrestle him, too, to the filthy floor, and to pry the ice pick out of his fingers.

Even so, the husband had killed the wrong lover, obviously!

The husband, with mounting excitement, had been following the wife all that morning, the ice pick clumsy in his pocket. The grocer's, the cobbler's, the butcher's . . . He did not know what he would do exactly until he found himself warm and breathless plunging into the fragrant calm of a florist's shop where, with trembling fingers, seeing with shame, as the salesgirl must have seen, his dirt-ridged nails, his scarred knuckles, he counted out nickels, pennies, for the purchase of a single stately long-stemmed rose of surpassing beauty. How long had it been, how many years, decades, since the husband had bought the wife any flowers, of any kind!—or even, as he'd once done, as a reckless young lover in an outlying district of Budapest, stolen some for her. As the wife passed unknowingly, arms laden with shopping bags, the husband stepped out of a doorway and fell in step beside her, quite astonishing the wife, who stopped, blinking, on the sidewalk, to stare. You! You *are* crazy, old man! the wife cried.

Before she could scold him further, the husband took the wife's bags and handed her the long-stemmed rose, which she accepted with a look of—how to describe it?—profound and rapturous surprise.

The butcher's was the nastiest bag, stained with rivulets of watery blood. The husband silently cursed, his hands would get sticky!

Now they were hurrying, the husband and the wife, uphill. Her arm linked through his. The long-stemmed rose bobbing in the wife's fingers. Both were breathing quickly, wincing. Their feet urged them onward, with the intemperate will of youth, but their shoes hurt their feet!—for both had bunions. A blush deep as the rose's petals lifted from the wife's neck into her plump face, and an identical blush mottled the husband's face. Their eyes glanced sidelong, shy and wondering. Where were they going, out of their familiar neighborhood? Who was taking them? A force like the wind pushed from behind.

There was a wrought-iron gate. A sudden moistly green grassy interior. Where?

The husband seized the wife's hand and pulled her inside, away from the noise and odors of the street. No! no! not here! are you drunk! the wife cried, squealing with laughter. Shopping bags lay tumbled on the grass. The husband laughed, and grunted, where he found resistance, pulling and tugging at the wife's clothes. Like eels they squirmed together onto the grass. Panting, pawing, the husband discovered what he had suspected—beneath the flesh-colored support hose, the wife was wearing sheer nylon stockings! with black seams! and beneath the old housedress a silky shift, the color of creamy magnolias! and, beneath that, the monster corset of canvas, cartilage, bone, nails—dozens of tiny hooks and eyes to be undone one by one if you had the patience not to tear, and rip, and the hell with it.

The wife's silvery-fair hair, loosed from its tight bun, fell rippling to her hips, as the husband had not seen it, by daylight, for a lifetime. How the husband's kisses stung, how his wiry mustache tickled!—how like reeling, drunken yellow butterflies their love cries lifted to the topmost leaves of the trees!

The ice pick, the ice pick, what of the ice pick? This, the husband set cannily aside, with his trousers, in the grass. For safekeeping. For, maybe, later.

Again, again! The husband had drunk himself into a stupor, had made himself sick! The wife, sobbing bitterly, hurried to the rectory of St. Matthias, where the priest's housekeeper, a countrywoman, allowed her, as she'd allowed her in the past, to use the telephone; as in the past, the wife called her eldest son, who did not live far away, after all. Would he come?—quick, quick, your father may be dying!—oh, please!

And so, sullen and dutiful, the eldest son left his home in the midst of supper, drove to the old neighborhood, ran up the ill-lit stairs, another time to confront his father who, in grimy undershirt and work trousers, insensible, raving, lay on the kitchen floor, a puddle of vomit at his head and, what was it?—an ice pick gripped so tight in his misshapen fingers, the son could not pry it out.

Oh Jesus, Mary, Joseph, oh what are we to do! What will become of us! the wife cried, beating her soft thighs with her fists, as the son squatted on his heels, struggling with the drunken man, and at last, with a fury of his own, wrenching the ice pick out of his grip by brute force. There was no answer to such questions, he was thinking—for who can see into the future?

The Mother

A long time ago when she was a girl she lay in secret with a photograph cut from a pulp-paper magazine smoothed carefully on the pillow beside her head, now she lies awake past midnight, past one o'clock in the morning, listening for her son to come home, waiting for the headlights to startle her skimming the ceiling and the noise of the tires in the gravel drive and the footsteps at the rear of the house that sound so shy and cautious. Then he will go to his room, he will close the door quietly behind him, she must imagine his warm flushed skin the bruised look of the mouth, the quivering eyelashes, eyes lidded with secrets, the smell of the girl on him which he won't wash off until morning, so many hours away. If she stares at him it must be in secret, he won't allow it otherwise, the soft down on his upper lip, the pale silky hair that is neither hers nor his father's, Why are you looking at me? Jee-suz!—but with a light nervous laugh, he isn't her baby any longer but a baby sleeps coiled up inside him, that deep clammy-still sleep of an infant whose breath you must check by leaning close, your ear turned to its mouth. The girls he sees don't wear lipstick so there won't be lipstick on his face, she can't allow herself to be angry.

Years ago she first turned a doorknob to discover it locked against her and she drew away frightened, ashamed, now she dreams of a hallway of doors locked against her, she calls out her son's name but no one answers, the voices are suddenly hushed, someone giggles softly, they were sitting atop a picnic table, her son and a girl she'd never seen before and whose name she did not know, she saw her son's arm slung about the girl's shoulders, she saw their heads nudging together, his blond hair gleaming bright as it did in a snapshot taken when he was nine years old. Do you think I don't know what you do with your girls, she whispered, do you think I can't guess? . . .

So many mirrors in the house, upstairs and down. But none shows her true face.

At meals the son and the father get along companionably, the son and the father and the mother, there is the exchange of news, there is chatter, laughter, both the men are good eaters which pleases the mother though even now, at his age, the son must sometimes be chided for eating too fast, and for dropping his head toward his plate.

Once she asked him why he was going out again so soon after he'd just come home, hadn't he been gone all day, at home for no more than forty minutes, why was he going out again, where was he going, she kept her voice light, calm, amused, in truth she *was* amused, it was so transparent, his lying. She saw how his eyes were hooded with secrets, how a pulse beat in his throat. She saw only that he wished to be gone since his life was elsewhere. She was pointing out that he'd been out late the night before, that it was raining, that he'd only just come home, it was all so childish, the game he played. A flush began in his face, that look of swallowed fury, shame, but she kept her voice light and unaccusing, she said, You're going to a girl's house, aren't you, please don't lie, isn't that where you're going, I'd like to know her name and I'd like to know if her parents are home and if they're not, I'd like to know if they know you're there, and though she was speaking calmly tears spilled from her eyes, her son backed away in shame, in embarrassment, in rage, as if he didn't trust himself closer to her.

Afterward every room in the house was a room he'd just slammed out of, the air was queer and sharp, as during an electrical storm, she saw her son's face growing smaller and smaller until the features were indistinct, she had to imagine the eyes, the set of the mouth, and cried out that he was so beautiful: so beautiful.

· · ·

She would smooth the photograph out carefully on her pillow and lie down beside it, carefully, not daring to breathe.

Rain blown against the windows, spilling noisily out of the gutters. The most secret time.

At night the father sleeps heavily while she waits for the flash of the headlights, the sound of the tires in the drive, minutes sliding into minutes, hours into hours, the father's breath is usually hoarse, rasping, dry, and only when he swallows it, when she becomes aware of an arrhythmic patch of silence, does she hear him, or, rather, she suddenly hears the silence, his terrible absence, like a heart that has ceased to beat. But in the next instant there will come a startled little snort, swallowed too, strangulated, and then with an air of surprise the breathing begins again, hoarse, rasping, dry, rhythmic, this too the absence of sound, to which she never listens. Why do you lie to me, she is saying to her son, her fingers closing about his arm as they have a right to close, her nails digging gently into his skin—do you think I don't know what your life is now? the things you do? you and your girls? you alone? in your room? with the door locked against your mother?

His fingers drum on a tabletop, his eyes shift in their sockets, so beautiful, the flush in his cheeks, the soft tawny down of the upper lip, even his raised aggrieved voice as he tells her to let him alone, for Christ's sake please let him alone. And the long sinewy legs, the muscular thighs, arms, the very set of the head, neither hers nor his father's. Who can claim him? Who can possess him? Who dares? She shuts her eyes against the boy and girl, those frantic young lovers, only partly undressed as they couple, eager, impatient, shameless, she hears the boy's life torn from him in a cry of deliverance, a cry of triumph, while she lies sleepless beside a sleeping man, waiting for release, waiting for his footsteps, the soft sound of a door being locked against her.

Sweet!

He was a long-limbed, husky child, hair the color of hot curry, with a narrow head, a low, bony brow, and rapt feral eyes set deep below the brow. The eyes were intelligent but quick-darting, watchful. His name was Thadius—an "ancestral" name of his mother's choice—but the child planned to have it legally changed as soon as he came of age. It was his vague expectation that, by that time, ten years away, his mother might have died.

He was growing, rapidly. Eleven years old, and growing.

Since the divorce, the child's mother had no news of his father to impart to others. Asked where the child's father was, she was apt to say, as if innocently, "why, he's flown the coop, like they all do—" pointing up into the sky.

The child, gnawing on a thumbnail, never asked. The father's imperfectly recalled existence was an embarrassment between the child and his mother like the awkward fact—the child assumed it was a fact: one of those truths we know without knowing how we know—that the obese sighing woman with the chin hairs he'd been encouraged to call Grandma as a little boy was now dead, had been dead for years.

Hard to imagine such a heavy woman having flown the coop, rising into the sky.

Since the father's departure, when Thad had been four years old, his mother had moved several times, always within the Buffalo

42

city limits but never within the same school district. By sixth grade Thad had stopped trying to learn teachers' and classmates' names—their faces too were blurred, inconsequential, like faces glimpsed from a speeding vehicle. It astonished him when these strangers gave evidence of knowing his name—calling out "Thadius!—Thad!"

He wondered if another boy, himself a stranger, stood where he stood. Another boy whom people saw, and seemed to know.

Thad's mother's maiden name was Chase, but she called herself "Mrs. Chase," to prevent, as she said, misunderstandings. It was an era of freedom for women, she told him vehemently. A woman has a child, and that answers God's wish, but, beyond that, living with a man, *that*—"There's no further need."

Thad was deeply embarrassed by such words as "woman" and "man" on his mother's lips, as if she'd said "shit" or "fuck" right there in the kitchen!

Mrs. Chase was a small, nervous, graying woman who worked some of the time as a salesclerk, downtown—"downtown Buffalo" was a region vast and romantic as a canyon in a western movie, enormously exciting to Thad though he had no true hope of ever being taken there—and whose preoccupations were her health and her religion. The child rarely looked directly at her, certainly could not have guessed her age, size, hair, and eye colors, yet whenever he saw Minnie Mouse in the comics he was reminded of his mother: Mrs. Chase was an older, disgruntled Minnie, with thin down-turned lips, staring protuberant eyes, an air of angry perplexity. She went each morning to six o'clock mass, taking Thad with her; she went frequently to the doctor—though "the doctor" was likely to mean numerous doctors. What girlish excitement in Mrs. Chase when she hurried off to be examined by a new doctor while still under the care of another!

She had respiratory weaknesses, and gastrointestinal weaknesses; she had dizzy spells, heart palpitations, gall bladder trouble; most consistently through the years, she had "female" troubles. When Thad was in fifth grade, Mrs. Chase was hospitalized three times during the school year. One of his teachers asked Thad what was wrong with his mother and the boy muttered, blushing, that it had "something to do with"—making a vague hooklike gesture toward his body.

The child's mouth trembled so, his teacher asked no further question.

Mrs. Chase accepted her various maladies stoically. She dosed Thad with cod liver oil, vitamin pills, brewer's yeast; she insisted upon twice yearly medical examinations; mother and son frequently went together to have their blood drawn for tests. Mrs. Chase said, "Jesus suffered, so we must, too," though she did not appear to be suffering but quite enjoying herself, and Thad said, sullenly, "*He* knew He was the son of God, that made it easier."

At such times Mrs. Chase might give a little cry of horror, and slap at Thad, who easily ducked away. "What! Talking like that! About *Him!*"

Thad muttered, "That's what He wants, isn't it? Everybody always talking about *Him?*"

Mrs. Chase's other activity was attending mass—or had been, until recently. She was a devout Catholic who had little interest in God or Jesus Christ apart from the Roman Catholic rites; and little interest in Roman Catholicism apart from the actual churches, the buildings, in which she worshiped. Yet, since Thad's ninth birthday, she'd gradually stopped forcing him to accompany her—the child was so restless, sitting in the pew, and so clumsy, genuflecting and kneeling, she feared the priests were annoyed by him; finally, surprisingly, she stopped going herself. She complained that God had stopped judging people—"There's no counting on Him anymore." Her small, pale, triangular Minnie-face screwed up in fastidious distaste.

Thad wondered in what ways his mother had counted on God, previously.

They moved so often, there was always a new apartment building and a new neighborhood to explore; or, as the child sometimes believed, it was the same apartment building and the same neighborhood, and he was a stranger, licensed to explore it.

Aged eleven, he spent much of his time alone, when not in school. He had no friends and made no effort to make friends; in fact, he seemed to have no interest at all in children his own age. Adults interested him, and girls. Sometimes he stared after them, frowning. His bright curry-colored hair was shaved up the back and sides of his head, emphasizing the disproportionate smallness of his head, and his eyes, which were recessed, furtive. He gave the impression of imagining himself invisible despite the fact that, five feet tall by the age of eleven, he was usually very visible, even in dim-lit corridors.

Seeing the child wandering in and out of apartment buildings in the neighborhood, tenants sometimes stopped him to ask what he wanted, who was he looking for, sometimes they were clearly hostile and sometimes they meant only to be helpful and always Thad quickly supplied a name—any name—several times pronouncing his father's name, or his own. "Never heard of him," he was told suspiciously. Or, "Nobody here by that name!" Thad one day got the idea of carrying a package or a paper bag, as if for a delivery; for instance, some bloodstained wrappings from the butcher's, folded around wadded paper. He discovered that if he walked briskly enough, and appeared to have a destination, people rarely gave him trouble.

By night, he scrutinized the lighted windows of the building to the rear.

Few of the tenants there took the time to pull their blinds, at least in their kitchens and living rooms; other rooms were more private, slatted in secrecy. (Though Thad could sometimes peer into these, too.) Couples—families—solitary men and women: Thad watched them compulsively, hanging out his window on the third floor, sometimes crawling out on the fire escape to get a better look. Across the space of a weedy, debris-cluttered backyard, these strangers seemed to lack identity, substance. Maybe they were in a dream—but whose dream? Sometimes, touched by a nearly unbearable excitement, Thad would shut his eyes, shut them very hard, and when he opened them, much time would have passed, it was late, very late, windows were darkened, the lives within them hidden.

How hard the child's heart beat!—as if in terror of extinction.

• • •

She lived on the first floor of the mustard-colored stucco building, across the weedy lot, and when she was home, when her windows were lighted, the child could look nowhere else.

A fleshy woman, with gleaming black hair twisted up around her head in a thick coil that, loosened, tumbled down her back and slithered over her heavy breasts in a way that made the child draw in his breath sharply. She appeared to live alone, must have had a job that allowed her to sleep late; she was careless about drawing her blinds, even in her bedroom. Even when she had a male visitor.

At first, Thad thought of her as faceless, even headless. Just the magnificent black snaky-shiny hair, the heavy breasts and thighs, the arms often bared to the shoulder.

He had no name for her, nor even any word. Thinking only, *There*.

He explored her building, calculating that her apartment must be 1-F. Leaning close to the door, he drew in a deep swooning breath. A smell of fried foods, a perfumy staleness. His groin stirred.

One day, seemingly by accident, he saw her face to face: *There!*

He'd been loitering in the foyer of her building and there she came pushing open the door, a grocery bag in the crook of each arm. It was a Saturday afternoon: blustery snowy: the woman was vexed by the trouble she was having, but good-natured, too, glancing at Thad as if she recognized him, a neighbor's child, perhaps, she made a pretty, pouting face, expelled breath in a whistle, and Thad stepped forward offering to help.

The most natural thing in the world. Good boy.

The woman smiled, as if she'd been expecting some help, from someone, and handed over one of the bags, a gratifyingly heavy bag stuffed with cans and bottles, and Thad followed behind her carrying it to her apartment at the rear, it *was* 1-F. He was enormously excited, his heart beat and kicked, he could not believe how easily this had happened, *Here I am: here.* Setting the woman's groceries down on a sticky kitchen counter amid a dizzying concentration of smells— cooking odors, perfume, hairspray. The woman's uncoiled black hair was more elaborate than he could have guessed, fastened with combs; her face was so striking—wide crimson mouth, spiky black eyes, dead-white powdered complexion—she might have stepped down from a billboard advertisement or a movie poster. She shrugged off her glamorous suede coat to reveal a full, shapely body—shoulders, breasts, waist, hips, thighs, legs, ankles—straining at the fabrics that contained it, profound as the contours of an exotic landscape. The child blinked and stared in a way that must have seemed comical to the woman, she was smiling at him, amused. She asked his name, and he mumbled a reply, and she said, "Ted?—*Todd?*" and he mumbled again, and she asked how old he was, and he told her, and she laughed heartily now, as if he'd said something funny, and riffled his hair, teasing, "E*leven*, that's all? You'd fooled *me*, sweetie!"

In his blind daze the child would have escaped then but the woman insisted upon giving him a tip. She extracted from the dense clutter of her purse—tight-packed as if with bodily organs, arteries, nerves—a snakeskin wallet, and extracted from the wallet a shiny fifty-cent piece, which she handed over to Thad, again a bit teasingly, saying, "Thanks—you're a sweet kid!"

The child saw his hand reach out dumbly, palm upward, to accept the coin. He was too stricken to thank her.

Fleeing, then, his face very warm, eyes lowered, damp. His head tingled where, so casually, carelessly, she'd touched him, drawing those long crimson-polished nails through his hair.

Does she know me?—who does she see, seeing me?

He crouched on the fire escape outside his window, in a light snowfall, shivering, peering down and across at the woman's windows. Late, late at night he kept a vigil, sick with excitement, prepared to scramble doglike back inside his bedroom, should anyone glance out at him.

Some nights, he was deceived. There were lights in the woman's apartment but she wasn't home. At other times, the blinds drawn, she *was* home, yet hidden from him, hardly more than shadowy movements that might have belonged to anyone. His groin stirred in perplexity and anger, like a living thing.

Like a snake, it was. At night, when he slept, it stirred with a sudden vehemence, waking him wide-eyed.

• • •

"Did you take a bath last night?—don't lie."

"Yes."

"Did you take a bath last night?—I said *don't lie."*

"Yes."

"The towel was wet, and the mat was soaked, and I heard the water in the tub—but you don't look clean: your hair is stiff with grease."

"No it isn't."

"Are you defying me?—I say it *is."*

"It isn't!"

She reached across the dinette table to touch his hair, and the child reared back from her with a little scream, and fled from the kitchen, overturning his chair in his haste. His mother called after him but he ran out of the apartment—out into the street.

Later staring at his head, his hair, in a mirror, his head, *his* hair, had the woman really touched him there?—raking her crimson-polished nails lightly across his scalp?

Sure, he washed his hair eventually. His mother kept after him, he hadn't any choice.

Her name was *N. Vecchia*—or *Vecchio*—she'd block-printed it in bright purple ink on a white card slipped into her mailbox slot. Thad peered at the name, peered into the narrow aluminum mail-box, but there was someone in the foyer eyeing him, he didn't linger.

Glimpses of her, on the street: in the suede coat, or a furry zip-up jacket, tight-fitting slacks, high-heeled shoes: the shoes made him stare, the heels were so high, teetering. Sometime she was alone and sometimes with a burly black-haired man named Mario—he'd over-heard her call him that: a name of power and virility—who was her most consistent man friend.

Hours in his darkened room. When he was supposed to be in bed. Staring, waiting. Her windows. Her lights, which were so random—unpredictable. He knew better than to go to bed and to try to sleep until the woman's lights were extinguished for the night, the row of windows down there finally darkened.

Unlike Thad's mother who lived a life of unswerving, chaste routine, the woman seemed to invent her life as she went along.

She was there, or she was gone. She might be home in the early evening, and Mario might arrive, they might eat together in the kitchen and then go into her bedroom where the blinds were likely to be drawn; she might be home in the early evening, dressing, brushing her hair, moving between bedroom, bathroom, kitchen chatting on the telephone or sipping from a can of beer, her robe carelessly tied, satiny undergarments showing, and then she'd be dressed, in spike-heeled shoes, and Mario, or another man, might arrive, and they would go out, and not return for hours—sometimes not that night. Or, she might come home briefly in the afternoon but disappear again, and all by daylight, so Thad was cheated of seeing clearly what was happening. How furious he was, gnawing at his thumbnail, at such times.

He'd prowl about the backyard, under cover of darkness. Peering into the woman's windows, if she'd left lights on; but since he stood on the ground, several feet below the windows, he could only look upward, at a sharp angle. Seeing ceilings. Seeing nothing.

A second time the child happened to be loitering in the foyer of the mustard-colored stucco building when the woman arrived breathless and vexed, grocery bags in her arms, and this time, too, quick, deferential, eyes lowered, he offered to help her; this time too she gave him, pressed into his moist, slightly trembling hand, a shiny fifty-cent piece. "Thanks! You're a sweet kid, y'know?" she said, teasing him with her slow bemused smile. It was warmer weather now and she was coatless, in a snug-fitting striped jersey dress, and gunmetal-gray stockings so shiny as to appear wet, and her hair was coiled and curled and affixed in place by rhinestone-studded plastic combs—the child stared at them as if counting. His knees were weak. His heart was beating erratically. In his groin, constricted by his cotton shorts, was that snaky-angry stirring, drawing the blood from his head.

The woman knew. Maybe she knew. Smiling at him, one side of her mouth lifted, slyly.

"You said your name's—Todd? *Ted?*"

"Yes."

Clutching the fifty-cent piece Thad backed away, fled.

·   ·   ·

The fifty-cent pieces he hid between the mattress and box springs of his bed.

And a rhinestone-studded red plastic comb—not the woman's, probably, but one he'd found in the weedy backyard, unexpected treasure.

One night, seeing the woman was home, in her bedroom, talking on the telephone, the child climbed down the fire escape, crossed to her building, and entered it from the rear. The first-floor corridor was empty. Like a dog guided by smell he went to the door of 1-F and tried the knob and, yes, it was unlocked.

Both times he'd helped the woman with her groceries, he'd noticed her door was unlocked.

Here I am. Here.

He wasn't sure she had not called him, sending her thoughts to him up in his room. Still, he had to be careful.

Walking on his toes to the doorway of the living room so he could see the woman not many yards away in her bedroom, sitting sprawl-legged on the edge of her bed, bare legs, dead-white legs, black satiny panties and a roll of fat at her waist and the sheen of her bra which was satiny black, too, and she was fussing with her hair, stroking it sensuously, talking with her friend on the phone, laughing—there was something about the woman's raucous tone, the child guessed she was talking to another woman.

And here I am. Where?

He waited. He had forever. The sensation between his legs was like a great coiled snake preparing to lunge but he knew to stand his ground, to simply wait. He listened, as the woman chatted, and he watched, he was memorizing without knowing he was memorizing as, sometimes, scanning his school textbooks, running his eyes down the columns of print and figures, turning the requisite number of pages assigned, he found he'd memorized without knowing or intending to do so—knowing only that it was something that happened, not invariably but often, and it happened *to* him, came from the outside.

Then the woman drawled good-bye, hanging up the phone, scratching the inside of her thighs with her polished nails, and the child woke from his trance and backed away, silently, his fingers swift and groping snatching up something from a table and slipping it in his shirt pocket and within seconds he was outside, safe in the night where no one could see him.

What was it?—an earring, a beautiful earring, copper hoops and turquoise, or plastic resembling turquoise, a five-inch dangling earring for a pierced ear.
Just to prove I was there.

In the night, the uncoiling angry snake. The hot sinewy length of him. The child was wakened, whimpering. A scalding heat had passed through him leaving him dazed, weak. When finally he had strength enough to rise from his bed to stagger to the window he saw, across the way, a single lighted window in the woman's apartment, a bedroom window, one or two slats of the blind jammed so he could see—almost—he *could* see—an unclothed female figure, headless, joined by another figure, similarly headless, with a dark, hairy torso and arms and then the window went dark, as if the interior had vanished.

He was carrying a bloodstained package but no one stopped him, in any case the door to the woman's apartment wasn't unlocked this time: he tried the doorknob quietly, but the door would not budge.

He was too excited simply to give up and return home so he left the building by the rear door and, since it was dusk, and maybe no one could see, or would see, he jimmied one of the woman's windows—a kitchen window—open, and climbed inside.

The bloodstained package, he tossed in a garbage pail. Wiping his sticky hands on the lid as best he could.

This time too he knew she was home, he'd seen her come in an hour before. Noiseless as a cat he tiptoed to the kitchen doorway and as he passed through the hall, which wasn't lighted, he saw, or, more precisely, his eye took in, a quick vision of the woman in the bathroom at the end of the hall, the door ajar, the woman seated on the toilet, a pink chenille robe falling open to show much of her naked breasts and covering her fleshsy legs only to midthigh, her

hair disheveled on her shoulders, mouth clean of lipstick distended
in a tremendous yawn—and in the living room the child stood very
still not breathing listening to a prolonged tinkle of water and the
toilet flushing and the woman's footsteps, heavy, barefoot, approaching him, and with a curious calm he would remember all his
life he simply stood rooted to the spot an expression on his freckled
face as of a blackboard hastily erased, not clean, but enough so that
the chalk marks have been obscured and are now indecipherable.

The woman, yawning, entered the room—saw the child—froze—
snatched at the front of her robe to close it—blinking at first in alarm,
then in annoyance, saying, "What the hell are *you* doing here?" and
Thad stammered, "I—I knocked on the door—I thought you said
'Come in,' " fumbling to draw out of his shirt pocket the earring with
the copper-turquoise hoops.

The woman stared. Then, relenting, "My earring?—where'd you
find it?"

Thad's face was hot, his groin painfully astir so he worried the
woman might notice. Her eye dropped to his feet, rose, took him in,
assessing. "On the sidewalk, I guess," he said. He gave the earring
to the woman, who took it from him as if doubting at first that it
was hers. She said, frowning, "Well. I'm glad to get it back—
thanks."

"Okay," Thad murmured, headed for the door.

There was a Yale lock on the door, similar to, though not identical with, the lock Mrs. Chase had on her door.

The woman stood barefoot, watching him. Though she wore no
makeup, her face was striking, the skin oddly shiny; her mouth
without lipstick looked unnaturally pale. "Just how'd you know
this earring was *mine?*" she asked.

"A lady told me, ma'am. Down the hall."

"What lady?"

"Fat lady. Down the hall."

Still the woman regarded him, thoughtfully. Her eye lingering on
him, bemused. Then she said, as if relenting, "Here's something for
you, kid—the earring *is* special." She sought out her purse in the
bedroom, to give him a tip.

While she was gone, Thad quickly adjusted the lock on the door.

As if, though intended to be locked, it hadn't quite caught—thus he'd been able to push the door open.

In any case, the woman noticed nothing. She was smiling when she returned, holding out a dollar bill to the child—"You *are* a kind of a sweetheart, eh?"

A dollar bill! Thad's eyes misted over. "Thank you, ma'am."

" 'Ma'am'? My name's Nicolette!" The woman laughed.

And riffled the child's hair another time, with rough affection, as, face burning, he stepped out into the hall.

How many nights following that did the woman send Thad her thoughts as he lay in bed, covers drawn over his head, heart beating slowly and painfully—he did not know. *My name's Nicolette. What the hell are* you *doing here? Sweet! Sweetheart.*

The thing between his legs stirred, thickened, came violently to life. The child groaned aloud. He dared not touch it for fear of scalding his fingers.

"What are you doing to yourself?—don't lie."

"Nothing."

"What?—I can't hear you if you mumble."

"Nothing."

"You look sick. You *are* sick. Don't lie."

"I'm not—"

"Above all things, *don't lie.*"

With an instinct for ferreting out secrets in their very hiding place, knowing where to look without knowing how she knew, Mrs. Chase marched into Thad's cubbyhole of a bedroom, threw back the bedclothes of his bed with a snort of disgust, then, further inspired, stooped to lift the mattress a few inches—to expose, to Thad's horror, the shiny fifty-cent pieces, the one-dollar bill, the rhinestone-studded plastic comb.

For a long moment mother and son stared at these objects. There was a profound silence.

Then Mrs. Chase glared up at her son with a look of triumph, and pain. "Thief! So that's what you are—a thief! *Don't lie!*" Before Thad could protest, she went on, "Did you steal these things at school?—in the building here?'' As he was about to speak, she said, half sobbing, ''A son of mine! A son of mine! A common thief! Oh, how could you! You're your father's son, after all! Aren't you! Aren't you!''

Thad watched mutely as his mother snatched up the fifty-cent pieces, the one-dollar bill, the rhinestone-studded comb—his little hoard of treasure. And then she let the mattress fall back into place with a hissing sound as of infinite contempt.

That rainy spring, the final week of school, he happened to see a stocky black-haired man descending the steps of the building in which Nicolette lived, Mario lighting up a cigar headed for his Olds parked at the curb, he watched as Mario gunned the motor, drove off in a cloud of exhaust. How quiet, then, how dull, the rain-washed street.

He hesitated only a moment. Then, as if his name had been called, he entered Nicolette's building.

Sweet! Sweetheart.

There was the matter of the door but he seemed to know the door would be unlocked. Mario, leaving, had been careless, yes Mario was a careless man, and Nicolette a careless woman, you could count on that. He tried the doorknob—pushed the door open. Was anyone watching?

Though it had been eight weeks since he'd been in the woman's apartment last, it seemed to him he'd never left it. *Here. I am here.* This time too the woman was in the bathroom—now taking a bath, splashing and singing to herself. Again the door was ajar, in fact the door was wide open. A steamy fragrance wafted about the child, quickened his heartbeat, aroused his groin so he had to tug at his trousers, in discomfort. The bathwater was warm, bubble-flecked, lapping over his bare belly, between his legs, tickling and caressing. *Here!*

He pressed close to a wall, gazing slantwise at Nicolette seated in the bathtub a short distance away—damp black hair pinned atop her head, heavy creamy-pale big-nippled breasts floating in the soapy water. She was singing, humming, to herself. Happily absorbed in her bath. Mario had just left, but she was not thinking of

Mario. She lifted one plump arm above her head, twisted about, doing what?—shaving her underarms!

The staring child shivered, feeling the razor blade scrape against the tender flesh of his own armpit.

He took advantage of the moment by crossing the hall into the bedroom, where the shades were still drawn. A dreamy sepia-slatted morning light fell upon the unmade, rumpled bed, the strewn-about clothes and shoes. Here the steamy fragrance was more concentrated, the child had difficulty breathing. His heart was beating so quickly he could see his chest palpitating.

A shoe was in his hand, suddenly—satiny black with a black velvet ribbon and a cheap gold buckle, three-inch heel, stiletto thin. The shoe gave off a sour, sweaty smell—the child shut his eyes in a swoon, smelling it.

When he opened his eyes he saw a digital clock on a table beside the bed: 8:56 A.M. He couldn't possibly get to school before the final homeroom bell rang. No point in trying.

She'd called him here, but was he certain? The shoe was proof.

Nicolette was still splashing in the tub, he'd be able to hear her if she rose, drained the tub. There was no danger of her discovering him if he was alert.

Here. Am I here?

He prowled the bedroom, sniffing like a dog. Blood beat fast in his temples—throat—belly—groin. No happiness like this! He knew, he knew. He didn't need a father to instruct him, nor any man. He poked his nose into every corner of the bedroom whose interior he'd imagined for so many months. The heel of the shoe was hooked in his belt like a trophy; when he left, he'd pull out his shirt to hide it. *Just to prove I was here. Am here.* He drew a wondering hand across the damp, sour-smelling bedclothes, he stooped to examine one of the pillows, which was smeared with lipstick as if the woman had gnawed it with her teeth. On a chair there lay a soiled nylon nightgown; underfoot, a lacy beige brassiere with enormous cups. Thad picked up something delicate, gauzy—peach-colored—a half-slip?—and pressed it against his burning face. He would have crushed it into his fist to shove into his pocket but at that moment he heard a sound behind him, a sharp indrawn breath, and, turning, he saw Nicolette in the doorway.

"You! Again! What the hell are you doing here?"

A naked woman—breasts, belly, pubic hair, cold cream smeared on her face like a mask, and her angry mouth caked with remnants of lipstick; eyes widened in disbelief. She had been drying herself with a thick blue towel which, now, she hastily clutched against the front of her body. She saw the shoe hooked in Thad's belt and advanced upon him, furious. "So that's it! *Thief!*"

Thad would have rushed out of the bedroom but Nicolette blocked his way. He was backing up—cringing—face burning with shame, guilt—an almost unbearable excitement—and he stumbled against the bed, and fell—and Nicolette was upon him in an instant, snatching the shoe out of his belt, striking him with it, cursing him. In her excitement she let the towel drop. "Oh you will, will you! You will, will you! Thief! Fucking little skunk!"— striking him with the shoe's sharp heel as he tried to crawl away. She stooped over him, grunting. She tore at his shirt, ripping it across the back, exposing his back—she tugged at his belt, yanked at his trouser legs. In a terror as of drowning the child saw her naked body above him, the pale, fatty-muscular legs unshaven above the knees, the flaccid skin of the belly, the bristling swirl of kinky black pubic hair lifting, in a swirl, faintly, to the eyelike little navel. The woman's breasts, the size of melons, swung loose as if enraged, too, brushing close to his head; her breath came short and heated; her enlarged, spiky black eyes glared at him as if through the eye slits of a mask. A powerful scent of bubble bath wafted from her spread, straining legs as she stood flat-footed, leaning over the bed, holding the child by his hair now as she struck his bare back and the tender tops of his buttocks with the heel of the shoe, again, again, hard enough to draw blood. What pain! What a whacking sound! The child whimpered and begged for mercy but there was no mercy, only a woman's triumphant cry in his ears: "Are you going to do this ever again! Are you going to do this ever again! Are you going to do this ever again!"

Forgive Me!

For expediency's sake I am writing this love letter to you, and to you, in duplicate, because there were two of you, D. and N., and neither of you knew of the other—that is, neither of you knew at the time that the other was also my lover—though you were friendly acquaintances, and both of you knew my husband to about the same degree.

Unless you, N., were a bit closer to my husband: you played handball together, didn't you? Now and then.

D., you rarely wasted time on athletics, if I remember correctly. Your aggression took more direct forms.

From one of you, I received this delicate jade ring which I wear sometimes—though not often: I have so many rings—on the smallest finger of my right hand. Was it a gift from you, D., or from you, N.?—forgive me for not remembering. Nineteen years is a long time in lives as crowded as ours.

From one of you, D., or N., I contracted a venereal infection—of a minor sort, cleared up after a single visit to my gynecologist and a two-week regimen of daily antibiotics. A sensation of burning and itching, nothing like the terrible venereal infections lovers transmit to one another these days!

N., you knew nothing of my relationship with D., though you seemed to be resentful of him, and jealous, as friends can be while remaining friends, a brotherly sort of intensity there, though not ever intimacy. I seem to remember an exchange of words between you at a party that, pressed a little further, would have become an argument: you, N., had seen you, D., and me, standing together in a corner of a room, talking earnestly, and you'd stared at us, and though it would not have crossed your mind (any more than it would have crossed your mind, D.) that there stood a sexual rival, and not merely the threat of one, you couldn't stop yourself from approaching us and interrupting.

What were the words, the skeins of impassioned, seemingly sincere, and always earnest words, we spoke in those days—or which spoke through us, in those days? As if we were musical instruments of some beauty and precision through which an ancient music played, without quite our knowing.

Between us—I mean between you and me, D., and between you and me, N.—there was frequently a sensation of utmost calm, as if violence were being restrained; as if two walls—two fields of quivering force—were pushing together, poised in perfect equilibrium. How happy we were, for all our misery!

Though you drank heavily, N.—and, as you acknowledged, drove your wife into therapy.

Unless that was you, D.—or both?

Nineteen years *is* a very long time.

After my husband and I moved away from that wind-tormented midwestern city in which we'd all been young, after my relationships with you both had subsided—as such relationships inevitably subside, innocently as wild fires dying out when they've consumed all there is to consume—we learned of course that our mutual friend K. had been a serious alcoholic for years without any of us knowing: how her death has lodged in me, to this very day! And when I think of that woman, her beauty on the edge of softening into middle age, I think of her posed smiling with a drink in her hand, a martini glass, I think, and there at her side might be standing you, D., or you, N., with drinks in your hands too—K. was so fond of you both, as she was fond of me. And never suspecting.

Alone of all of you in those days I did not drink, and felt awkward, apologetic. I stood on shore as the ship of gaily chattering and laughing men and women with drinks in their hands set out for sea, leaving me behind. So my laughter had to grow shriller, to compete.

I think I can remember the winter day I fell in love with you, D.—we were walking somewhere, stamping at the snow, and you looked at me in a certain way, helpless, with such desire, I felt my heart swell with happiness. And your infatuation for me, N., had probably prepared me for this moment: gave me the confidence I would not have had otherwise. Such happiness, such misery, forgive me!—I couldn't resist.

Which of you meant more to me, I can't remember. I would guess that my feeling for you shifted from day to day, virtually hour to hour, as such feelings invariably do. And there was my husband, too, so much superior in character, or in what might be called the soul, than the three of us.

So on this nineteenth anniversary of one or another of our desperate hotel afternoons, when death seemed the only way out, and our tears ran together, I am sending each of you a love letter: forgive me for my economy, in sending you each the same one.

Which of you broke my heart, and caused me such humiliation, I can't remember. Unless it was I who broke your hearts, in duplicate.

Sometimes I'm haunted by a single memory: you, D., bending over your youngest daughter, the one with the curly red-gold hair, you were wiping her nose, teasing her, and she was looking up at you, and I stood a few feet away watching, something too naked in my face because when you glanced up to see me you were visibly nervous, worried I might blurt out something, in those days I was passionate, or believed I should be, a beautiful woman because so many men had assured me, yes, yes, you are, but it was your child's beauty that astonished me, so for a long long moment I simply stood staring at her, in homage to her. And that was all.

Or was that beautiful little girl with the red-gold curls your daughter, N.?—forgive me, I've forgotten.

Transfigured Night

Midway in the string sextet performance of Schönberg's "Transfigured Night" the husband shifted restlessly in his seat and leaned over to inform his wife that he was leaving: he had work to do at home, he couldn't concentrate on the music, he was bored. The wife protested in a whisper, "You can't leave me alone—how would I get home?" "Leave with me," said the husband. "Or take a cab." He did not wait for her reply but got to his feet, stumbled over legs, strode up the aisle with his trench coat slung over his shoulder. The wife stared after him, astonished. She could not believe that her husband of seventeen years—by nature so courteous, even gentle—the most reasonable of men—had behaved with such rudeness! And in so public a place!

Dazed, she remained in her seat for the duration of the Schönberg piece, but without hearing a note; managing, by the end, to convince herself that her husband would be waiting for her in the lobby. It was unthinkable really that he would go home without her. But at intermission she did not find him amid the crowd of concertgoers. Not in the lobby, not on the building's front steps, not in the parking lot where their car had been parked. For some minutes, her eyes welling with tears of hurt, anger, and humiliation, the wife wandered through the lot as if searching for their car . . . though she could see plainly that the space in which it had been parked was now empty.

And yet—was it possible? Her husband who loved her, and whom she loved, an intelligent, civilized man, had treated her so boorishly?—had left her behind to fend for herself? Not once in their long association had he done anything like this.

Walking slowly and haltingly as if wounded, in the direction of a nearby hotel where taxis were likely to be available, the wife glanced up repeatedly at passing cars, convinced that one of them would be theirs. But none was. She felt exposed and helpless as an abandoned child.

There must be some explanation, she told herself. Some misunderstanding. A serious problem, perhaps—professional? emotional?—her husband was confronting alone, having wanted to shield her from it. Otherwise—she couldn't comprehend his behavior.

Several taxis were queued up beside the hotel's front entrance, but the sight of the drivers congregated on the sidewalk, smoking, talking loudly together, laughing—stocky men with caps and cigars who might have been brothers—was daunting to the wife; she hesitated to approach them. She knew that as soon as she moved into the sphere of their attention, they would break off their jocular conversation and regard her silently; the cluster of them united in their maleness. One would murmur something and the others might laugh, underhandedly, even derisively. She could not bear it.

So she continued on and crossed the street farther up the block, thinking to enter the hotel from the rear. She could telephone a friend and ask to be driven home. She could, if she wished, take a room in the hotel for the night. That would chastise her husband, if she stayed away overnight, and he didn't know where she was. . . . Would he notify the police? Would he care at all?

She pushed her way impetuously through the hotel's revolving doors but paused just inside the entrance, staring at the crowd of well-dressed men and women in the lobby. They were people very like herself and her husband. She was transfixed with shyness: she dreaded seeing someone she knew, for how could she explain her situation? What *was* her situation? Alone, on foot, without her husband, without her car? Three miles from her home in the suburbs, on a Saturday evening? And dressed as she was in her black cashmere coat with the sable collar, and her new calfskin high-heeled shoes! Carrying a black satin embroidered evening bag! Pearls screwed into her ears but her hair windblown and her eyes glistening with tears of shock and mortification!

She'd been married for so long, she realized she was conditioned to being in certain parts of the city exclusively with her husband, particularly after dark. How unnatural, even ungainly, it seemed, to be alone!

She found herself out on the street again, walking blindly . . . not knowing what she would do. She felt as if every car in passing scrutinized her; in a moment she might be jeered at; yet at the same time, being a mature woman, intelligent, as rational in her expectations as (she would have said) her husband, she understood that her situation was certainly no emergency and might be coped with if only she could think. A taxi was certainly a possibility, and a hotel room for the night, and a quick pleading call to a friend—though did she dare trust even her dearest friend? wouldn't her humiliating story be known to everyone in her circle within twenty-four hours? The thought came to her suddenly: "Walk home."

Walk home. The idea was preposterous but somehow cheering: she *would* walk home. She had never walked home in all her years of living here and she was scarcely dressed for a hike of three miles and the air was blowsy and tinged with rain, but this seemed to be the alternative that, oddly, most appealed. Her husband would be astonished at her independence. She would astonish herself. She had her own key to the house and she would simply slip inside, quietly—the house half belonged to her after all. In the event of a divorce it might become hers entirely.

So, walking at a brisk pace, the wife set out for home. It was not yet 9 P.M. The streets were well lit and fairly populous. By degrees the sullen stab of her heartbeat became less painful, more like the heartbeat of excitement. Her eyes cleared. How vivid everything looked! Nimbi of moist light trembled at the edges of objects and far overhead, windblown, moonlit, the sky was in tatters. She could not sing to herself the wordless haunting melody of Schönberg's "Transfigured Night"—it was too elusive and dissilient to her untrained ear—but she sang familiar songs as they came to her: "My Heart's in the Highlands," "That Old Black Magic," "The Battle Hymn of the Republic."

It wasn't long, however, before the sidewalk abruptly stopped. The well-lit city street became a suburban road, semirural, posted at forty-five miles an hour, leading out into the night. The wife was then forced to walk on the edge of the pavement, a tricky and possibly dangerous tactic since the road was not wide, and, dreading oncoming headlights that would expose her, she chose to walk with her back to traffic. But if she walked on the shoulder of the road her heels quickly sank into the soft gravelly earth.

A light rain was falling, feathery and cold.

After some minutes the wife realized she wasn't singing any longer. The air was deathly still.

Then a car approached, its headlights blinding. The wife instinctively shielded her face. Please don't stop for me, she begged, but indeed the driver braked to a quick stop. A man called: "Hello! Is something wrong? Did your car break down?" At least, the wife thought, it was no one who knew her. She shook her head and said no, nothing was wrong, nothing at all—"I'm just out for a walk." The man persisted: "Would you like a ride somewhere?" and the wife said, more firmly, no, no, she would not; walking on; not wanting to be rude but desperate to get away. And the car drove off.

But to her dismay another car appeared almost at once. When it too showed signs of stopping the wife ran up a stranger's graveled driveway—in so doing stumbling and turning her ankle. "Oh! God!" The first stab of pain was excruciating. She waited, panting, until the car had passed, then returned, limping, humbled, to the road.

She would never forgive her husband for this ordeal.

She would hear no explanations from him, no excuses however heartfelt and sincere—she would never forgive him.

Her ankle throbbed so, she could hardly walk. Her heels were chafed raw by her tight-fitting shoes. For some reason the lower part of her spine ached. There was a 7-Eleven store at an intersection close by and the wife decided she had no choice—she'd go to it, and call her husband, and ask him please to come get her. She was after all halfway home.

Making the call, however, was not so easy. On the first try the wife misdialed the number and got a recording from the telephone company instructing her to dial again. On the second try, listening to the ring at the other end, she suddenly could not bear it—she replaced the receiver as if it were afire and burning her fingers.

She despised him! She wanted a divorce!

And what if he refused to come get her?

She was standing in a sort of daze in the store's fluorescent glare when the door exploded inward and a tall big-bellied man in a windbreaker entered. He must have been six feet five; two hundred twenty pounds; unshaven; with small fierce suspicious eyes pouched and ringed like a raccoon's. He wore soiled work trousers and a sheepskin-lined windbreaker with a broken zipper and a hunter's Day-Glo orange cap pulled down on his bushy gray hair. A man in his early fifties whom the wife recognized: hadn't he done some tree work for her husband, years ago, when they'd first moved into their house? Fortunately, he didn't seem to recognize her but walked on heavily by. He threw his weight on his right leg and dragged the left as if it were partly paralyzed.

On his way out the man in the windbreaker joked with and teased the teenaged cashier until the girl exploded in fits of high-pitched giggling. The wife felt a stab of envy; for no one of course in her life would ever so joke with and tease *her*; at the same time she was repulsed as if forced to witness an act of intimacy. She went outside and stood in the slow-falling rain. What was she doing here? How had this happened? High overhead enormous rainclouds were shifting about the sky like ancient galleons.

"Ma'am? You waitin' for someone?"

The man in the windbreaker—the wife remembered his name: Panacek—was standing beside her. His breath smelled strongly of beer. He carried several packs of beer in his arms. "You look like a lady in need of a ride somewhere, or something," he said. He spoke, for all his bluster, with a curious veiled formality.

The wife feared to look him in the face, for what if he recognized her? She started to say politely, "Thank you, but I'm perfectly fine, I'm waiting for my husband to pick me up," but instead she burst out, "I'm afraid to go home!"

And began sobbing uncontrollably.

From approximately 9:45 P.M. until 11:30 P.M. they drove in Pana-cek's mud-splattered pickup truck along country roads in which farmland and wooded areas were interrupted by residential develop-ments with such names as Fox Hollow, Beechwood Park, and Pheasant Ridge Park; once they approached the winding unpaved road—Cold Soil Lane—where the wife herself lived, a mile and a half away. The landscape, alternately illuminated by moonlight, then darkened by clouds, was both familiar and utterly alien to the wife, who stared at everything like a blind woman suddenly forced to see.

The truck was a 1977 Ford, badly rusted, smelling inside of oily rags, Panacek's sweat, and wet dog hair, though there was no dog in the truck. Helping the wife climb in—she'd still been sobbing as if her heart would break—Panacek had mumbled, "Th'ow that stuff that's on the seat in the back, ma'am, an' watch out for your stockings." As he drove Panacek drank one beer after another, slowly and meditatively, and insisted that the wife drink, too, so she too held a can but hardly dared sip from it for fear of spilling beer onto her coat. The unpaved roads were rough and Panacek drove them with an easy familiarity and the wife's hand was trembling slightly in any case. When Panacek had introduced himself he'd said, "I'm Herman Panacek," and looked the wife full in the face and she'd said shyly and evasively, "My name is—" giving not her first name, but her middle name and no last name at all. Panacek was too bluff and hearty, maybe a little too drunk, to note these subtle distinctions, or so the wife believed.

Panacek drove aimlessly, and talked. The wife—known to him as "Carol"—sat silent beside him as if mute, very still, stiff, staring for the most part straight ahead. Panacek told her about the area as he remembered it from forty, forty-five years ago when he'd been a child, most of it farmland and some of it just unclaimed and wild, and then with the war things changed, and in the last decade things *really* changed. The developers who'd built up the town began to take their hot-shot operations into the country; farmers began sell-ing off their land; fancy split-level ranch houses and colonials and places with outdoor swimming pools began to appear down the road from old farmhouses nobody with a grain of sense would want—and nothing was ever the same again. Of course Panacek had profited, too. He had a tree service, no millionaire deal but he did okay, rich people were always anxious to spend money on their lawns, having

their trees trimmed, cut down, topped, whatever—"The more
money the bigger the asshole."

Panacek laughed, belching beer, then said, "No offense, ma'am?
I mean, if your husband's—?"

"Oh no," the wife said quickly. "No offense."

She was shivering with cold though it wasn't at all cold in the
truck—Panacek had turned on the heater to warm her.

"You'd best tell me what is happening in your life, Carol,"
Panacek said finally, "if you want some help." "Oh no, I don't
want any help!" the wife said. "That's up to you," Panacek said
gravely. "I don't ever butt my nose in where I'm not wanted." "Oh
no, I don't want any help," the wife said, "it's just that I'm afraid
to go home tonight." She paused, wondering if this were true. "Or
any other time," she added. "Well," said Panacek, whistling thinly
through his teeth. "Well well *well*."

He reached out to stroke her shoulder, her hair. His big calloused
fingers brushed against her cheek. She sat very still. She did not
breathe. Overhead the moon's eerie light sliced through a crevice of
cloud with a little cry of pleasure. The wife heard herself say
quietly, "Something happened to me tonight that has changed my
life forever, my marriage." Panacek said, "And what was that,
Carol?" The wife said, "Oh, I can't say." Panacek said, "Did the
son of a bitch raise his hand to you? Did he hurt you? Eh?" The wife
drew breath to deny this but burst into tears instead. Panacek
braked the truck to a stop and switched on the light and asked again
if her husband had hurt her and where and not exactly knowing
what she did, trusting as a child, the wife lifted her leg to show him
her bruised ankle.

Again Panacek whistled thinly through his teeth. He seemed
never to have looked upon such a wound. "Christ! *He* do that? *Kick*
you?" he asked incredulously.

He caressed her ankle reverently; held it in both his hands for a
long tense tender moment. "Maybe I'll have a little talk with him,"
he said.

"Oh no," the wife said quickly, "my husband is a violent man."

Why did I say that? she wondered. Not once during the seventeen
years of their marriage had her husband struck her or touched her

in anger; indeed, he'd rarely raised his voice to her, and she had rarely raised hers to him. She added, confused, "I mean, he's a sensitive man. He'll be upset."

Panacek laughed. "That's how it is, is it?"

He reached grunting beneath the driver's seat and pulled out a tire iron. "What is that?" the wife asked. "Tire iron," Panacek said. "Oh," said the wife faintly. "For protection," Panacek said. "Oh. I see," said the wife, staring.

Panacek laid the tire iron on the seat between them carefully and started up the truck. "Cold Soil Lane, you said?—that's right close by." The wife said, "Oh, I don't know—I don't think we should go there. I don't—" "This time a few years back, hell, it was a lot of years back, I was just out of the marines drivin' somewheres along the shore mindin' my own business and it's summer, see, and my window's rolled down, and I'm just drivin' along mindin' my business and some cocksucker tries to cut me off at a traffic light but I get ahead of him. An' at the next light he comes up beside me an' I wasn't even watchin' an' this son of a bitch buddy of his in the passenger's seat leans over with some kind of a straight razor and cuts my arm when they go by—cuts my fuckin' arm from about the elbow up to the shoulder and Christ did I bleed like a stuck pig! I mean," Panacek said, laughing loudly, "did I *bleed!* Took seventy stitches to sew me up an' I made a promise to myself I always kept afterward that Panacek'd never be a sittin' duck like that again. Anybody touches me I'm goin' to touch the fucker right *back.*"

He spoke heatedly and excitedly, yet with an air of amusement.

The wife picked up the tire iron and weighed it in her hand. She had never lifted a tire iron before. "It's heavy," she admitted. "It'll do the job," Panacek said. "What job?" the wife asked. "Any job that's required," Panacek said. They were driving along a country road that looked familiar to the wife though she could not, as in a dream, have named it. And then when Panacek turned onto Cold Soil Road she did not seem to recognize it immediately. "Which house is yours, Carol?" Panacek asked, squeezing her hand. "The last one on the left where there's an outside light burning," she said, and added, "But you don't need to come inside with me." Panacek laughed, saying, "No trouble, ma'am." The wife said, stammering slightly, "No, really, Mr. Panacek, you don't need to come inside with me." Panacek said, "You don't think so, eh? That's how it is, is it?" The wife could not think how to reply. She looked at Panacek and saw that he was smiling at her, and she tasted cold, but she could not think how to reply.

They drove the rest of the way in silence.

Actress

She must have expected to hear from him, or at least of him, since when her assistant brought her the telephone message, she was not surprised.

Or, at any rate, she did not express any surprise.

She *was* an actress, after all. Forty-eight years old: yet more beautiful, and a far better actress, than she'd been eighteen years ago, when she'd left this city.

Then, she'd led a wayward and hopeful life. Now, she was a virtuoso of emotion she not only did not feel, but could not, in truth, take altogether seriously. And where there might be spontaneous emotion of her own, for instance apprehension, or eagerness, or dread, or surprise, the actress was no more likely to express it involuntarily than a mask is likely to suggest any affect other than the one etched into its surface.

So: on the afternoon of her opening of a three-week run of Chekhov's *The Seagull* in this midwestern city in which, years ago, she'd lived for the better part of a decade, her assistant brought her a telephone message from the man with whom, in the actress's imagination, the city was inextricably bound; and the actress read the message quickly, with her usual air of distraction that veiled an intense absorption in all things that touched upon her, and said, "But I don't know who 'R' is—if he calls again tell him 'There's no reply.' "

"Should I say you hadn't received the message yet, you've been out, or should I say you don't intend to reply?"

The actress, who always chose her words with care, as if they were scripted for her, thus impersonal, crystalline, repeated: " 'There's no reply.' "

Did the actress have an extraordinary talent for memorizing words, or had her extraordinary talent for memorizing words developed in tandem with her craft as an actress?—for in those two or three seconds when she'd skimmed the telephone message from R., written in her assistant's schoolgirl hand, she had memorized it. Involuntarily.

Are you ever nervous before a performance? Do you ever forget your lines? Why have you concentrated on theater, not films? What advice would you offer to young people who hope for careers in acting? Is it as cruel and competitive a life as people think? You've said that Chekhov is your favorite playwright, beyond even Shakespeare— which roles have you played, and why do you place Chekhov so high? You're said to be a thoroughly professional actress, respected and admired by theater people—would you have preferred popular fame? Would you live the same life again? Would you have done anything differently? I see by the program notes that you once played Nina in The Seagull, *and now you're playing Arkadina, a much older woman, and in fact a successful actress—how does that feel? Or are you accustomed to that sort of thing by now?*

The message from R. on the little notepad embossed with the name and logo of the elegant hotel in which the troupe was staying was not torn angrily into pieces but, simply, folded neatly into smaller and smaller squares, reduced to approximately the size of one of the Concord grapes in the lavish cornucopia of fruit, candy, champagne, and flowers in the actress's sitting room, and dropped into a wastebasket. And though the actress had memorized the message she felt no need to replay it in her memory, nor to give it, or R., any further thought.

Except as she walked through a city park (vigorously, as she always did, for no less than thirty minutes daily) fragments and particles of other, earlier words drifted into her consciousness, raised like grit by the gusty wind off Lake Michigan and, like grit, blown almost immediately away. *You know I will love you forever, yes, I know, how can you doubt me, but yes yes I know, I can't live without you, I couldn't bear it how could anyone bear it . . . without a soul. How?* The actress wore trousers, a jacket with wide sporty shoulders, her silvery blond hair in a rope wound around her head and covered with a silk scarf, dark glasses with chunky white plastic frames should anyone recognize her, and no one did *for which thank God.*

She was thinking, not of R., nor even of the words that were blown through her head, but of the fact that, yes indeed, the actress had once played the silly young ingenue Nina and was now playing the mature, worldly, self-assured Arkadina, an actress of reputation, who exclaims, perhaps carelessly, to Nina, "You simply must go on the stage!"

And so I did. And so, yes . . . I did.

Maturity consumes the hopes and energies of youth. But also youth's stupidity.

The company had been on the road for nine weeks now, San Francisco, and Houston, and now Chicago, and next Detroit, and each opening night was still an "opening," an occasion for commingled dread and euphoria, the usual. In any city the actress visited in this phase of her life, the actress received telephone messages, telegrams, personal letters left at hotel desks, often flowers, chocolates, other tokens of esteem. And requests for interviews: local newspapers, local television, and radio stations. To some of these she replied personally, to others her assistant replied, always courteously, always thoughtfully, for you must never never allow another person to know or even to suspect that the value he might wish for himself cannot be granted him, at least by you, at least at this time.

Of course I'd live the same life again—what a question!

Otherwise, who on earth would be standing here, in my place?

And these lines and shadows in my face—don't you think I've earned them?

·   ·   ·

And then it was time to go to the theater, virtually across the street from the hotel, and then it was curtain time, and once again the actress inhabited her role as seemingly without effort as she wore her costume, for she had no need to simulate Chekhov's Arkadina, she *was* Arkadina, at least for the duration of the performance. Not once did she allow herself to glance out into the audience *was he there? was she at risk, if he was? suppose without meaning to she glimpsed his face?—suppose after so many years it was scarcely recognizable as* his *face?* nor did she look for him backstage or at the stage door *where it would not be likely he'd be waiting, in any case: not R.*

The opening night was a huge success. The protracted applause was lovely, if expected.

Backstage the director confided in the actress that her costar'd been a bit lazy, in his opinion, but she'd been superb, she'd carried them all along. As one who craved praise, at least from her fellow professionals, the actress did not feel comfortable in hearing it but seemed as always distracted, embarrassed, repaying compliments with a knowing smile: "Aren't you sweet to say so!"

R. had been one of those, but only one, who'd complained that she'd deflected love, too, in this way. On this point the actress could not offer any judgment since she had not the slightest idea what such a death sentence might mean.

. . . it's as if the role exists beforehand, in a compartment of my mind, like a room I can enter; and as if life is a sequence of rooms, one leading into another, like an ingenious Belasco backstage, except the final room has only three walls, the fourth is gone, there's space where an audience is sitting . . . and in this final room, called a "stage," all that one is is one's effect upon others.

I've never given it much thought, but I suppose it's . . . strange. Normal people have little consciousness of their effect upon others, but that's all the actor is concerned with: effect.

It could be said, the actor doesn't exist. Only his or her effect upon an audience exists.

In the supper club where they celebrated afterward, jammed into cushioned leather booths, devouring champagne, pâté, oysters, steak sandwiches, omelets luscious with morel mushrooms, the actress endured a good deal of exclamatory praise, and said finally, not knowing quite what she said, "If I was halfway effective to-night it was because . . . I was playing against an adversary."

The actress would have secretly preferred to return at once to her hotel room and go to bed and sleep and sleep and sleep, but here she was, unaccountably, drinking with the others another time, fatigued, giddy, uproarious with laughter, susceptible to slivers of melancholy, even chagrin, *who knows why? symptoms of the trade*, determined not to drink more than three glasses of champagne, delicious as it was. One of the young men asked her what did she mean by an adversary, was it one of them, and she said quickly, "Of course not," wondering why she'd blundered onto so intimate a subject, "you're my friends. I meant an adversary in the audience."

"The audience itself, or just an individual?"

"I'd rather not talk about it."

"But what you're saying is so strange—who was it?"

With a silvery peal of laughter the actress threw up her hands. The fingers were beautifully tapered and beringed, the nails meticulously manicured and buffed. "Oh, I don't know!" the actress said. "I seem to be talking nonsense . . . I must be drunk."

Still the young man persisted, watching her closely. "But who was it? An old enemy? An old friend? Did you actually see him in the audience? Did he say he'd be there? Did he warn you—threaten you?"

Suddenly the actress got to her feet.

"No one threatens *me.*"

It was late, past one o'clock in the morning . . . truly she was exhausted.

There were extravagant good-nights, handshakes, hugs, and kisses, further praise, and Arkadina's Trigorin lurched to his feet, reiterating the pleasant fact that the actress had been wonderful that night, she'd carried them all with her, and he embraced her so hard the breath was knocked out of her; and she felt a tremor of something like physical fear where once, not so very long ago, she would have felt a powerful erotic jolt.

"Aren't you sweet to say so."

•   •   •

May I see you? Tonight, after the play? Or tomorrow? Any time,
really: please call. R.

In her king-size bed with its absurd number of pillows the actress
lay in a state suspended between wakefulness and sleep. It was the
fault of the dark, which was inadequately dark. And of something
she'd too greedily devoured with her perfectly white-capped teeth.
And of a fragrance in the room—lilac, lily-of-the-valley.

Her heart beat slow and hard in triumph.

There's no reply.

None? Nothing? No reply?

No reply.

If he'd been out there in the audience amid the rows and rows of
applauding strangers, the actress had not glimpsed him; in fact, she
had not looked. As if the fourth wall were there, opaque and inviolable after all.

Oh—very likely he hadn't even been there: he'd have waited to
hear from her, expecting a complimentary ticket; two complimentary tickets. For himself and his wife, if he was still married.

The actress began to hear the tumultuous applause, a waterfall of
applause, bringing a blush of gratitude, and gratification, to her
cheeks. Oh yes! Oh yes—certainly! Yes, you are loved, how could
you doubt *us!* And finally she fell asleep, stupefied by sleep,
bemused and then a bit annoyed by another presence in the bed
. . . a selfish sort of presence, crowding her.

How was it possible? She knew she was alone, of course.

Still the other body, the weight, the presence, nudged against her,
warm and persistent: against the length of her thigh, her back, her
legs. She was angry, exasperated . . . amused. Hadn't he enough
room of his own! Sometimes her hair had trailed over his face,
waist-long hair it had been, and he'd snorted and wheezed in play
. . . coiled a strand of it around his very neck, in play. And there
were his feet, his so strangely chilled feet, nudging hers.

The actress shook with laughter, thinking suddenly of feet. The
bareness of feet, toes . . . their vulnerability, their somehow comical
intimacy. Never do you think of feet in quite this way at any other
time, except this time.

The False Mirror

For E. and E.

They were in London, their city of dreams, even in its less idyllic aspects a place of enchantment: the squares, the parks, the embankment, the antiquarian book stalls, the pubs and theaters and museums, Chelsea Walk, where, one sabbatical year when they were very young, they'd rented a flat overlooking the Thames.

Every Sunday they went out to brunch and made a ritual of reading all the newspapers, and so they were now at an outdoor cafe near their hotel (just off Bloomsbury Square this time), and the husband went to buy newspapers from a vendor and brought several back to their table, peering at headlines. The wife took one of the papers from him and began to read, then looked up, suddenly, and said in a sharp voice, "This isn't real! We aren't really in London. This is a dream." The husband smiled uncertainly, supposing she must be joking, saying, "What? A dream?" And the wife said, trying to remain calm, "Because if we were really in London, we would already have bought this—" indicating a copy of *Time Out*, which indeed it was their practice to buy before the weekend. The husband said, "Of course this is real, look how real it is," glancing about the cafe, and the wife said, reaching instinctively for his hand, "No, it only seems real, it must be a dream," and to humor her the husband squeezed her fingers reassuringly, saying, "We're real, obviously—*I* am," and the wife shook her head slowly, anxiety building in her voice: "Do you think so? It seems real, but maybe it isn't. Maybe—'' And they were both looking around intently at the familiar setting, for the cafe was one of their favorites for Sunday brunch, yet was there something not quite right about it?—the faces of the other diners, their movements, the positioning of their bodies?—the murmurous background of voices, motors?—the sky clotted with chalky clouds in a too uniform pattern, like wallpaper? They were holding hands tightly, for this at least was incontestably real, their marriage of nearly thirty years the one absolute certainty upon which each could count, and one said, in a voice meant to convey hope, though not without an undercurrent of bemusement, "Maybe if we wait, we'll know," and the other said, "But how long, do you think, will we have to wait?"

From *The Life Of . . .*

The Great Man is introduced to applause. Applause swelling and washing over him. He tries to breathe. He tries to speak. "An honor," he says with an inward nip of his mouth. Most of the audience is hidden behind blinding lights, but he can see isolated faces—men, women—strangers—and he can see the joy shining wetly in their eyes. "An honor," he whispers. "I have waited so long." He is elderly, it seems. His muscles have turned to string, folds of flesh droop from his underjaw. Nonetheless he holds his head high. His tuxedo front, briskly starched, holds his torso in place. There is a chill wind from out of the east, a hint of lunar night. Beyond the rows of seats the Earth curves off gently into darkness. The Great Man waits in terror for the applause to die down, yet he is impatient, too. He has always been impatient, otherwise he would not be the Great Man but a man like any other.

Where once, in the distant past, Unreality sometimes intruded, and was jarring to his soul, now, sometimes, Reality intrudes when it is neither expected nor desired, and is jarring to his soul. For instance—biographers, take note—the neon-bright green of a slice of kiwi fruit on his plate at this noon's ceremonial lunch; his wife's raw, throaty, startled laughter where he had expected only silence; a harp's liquid-smooth waterfall notes, dipping and turning, rising, floating, Oh, please take me with you, piercing the buzz and babble of a hotel lobby. Had he thought his soul was dead, awakening is such a shock? . . . Your "soul!" Your "fine-honed sensibility!" whispers his wife, who knows him well, but his wife is not here, indeed she isn't here, not to regard his glistening forehead with anger and anguish and to swipe at it with a handkerchief, old fool! old lecher! at your age! while the old fool and lecher stands in abashed silence. In a gilt-mirrored elevator rising to the Xth floor the Great Man is to be observed mumbling lines from Shakespeare, Richard III in his final passion, "What do I fear? Myself? There's none else by; Richard loves Richard, that is, I am I."

The Great Man is being interviewed on television. He's happiest so. Where else can he deliver himself to be redeemed? A tiny plastic microphone clipped to his vest, he's wired for sound, to what do you attribute your greatness, sir, when did you realize you were the hero of a special destiny, sir, and it keeps him young and trim—wavy white hair brushed back from his forehead, mustache full and snowy, the ease of a practiced smile, Give me a breast to suck, give me Rilke's "green of real green." Two cameras hover over him and will outlive him, the Great Man captured for what remains of eternity. I craved greatness and greatness like lava flowed over me. Golden lava, gentlemen! ladies! Golden! Golden! Do you know what that means? Always afterward he's congratulated, his hand is shaken, it's still a strong hand strong steely fingers and don't forget it.

The Great Man stands alone at the rear of the hotel lobby listening to a female harpist playing Debussy, Ravel, Schubert. The hotel is small, elegant, "European," a place of deep-piled crimson carpets, salmon pink sofas and cushions. The Great Man has been registered here incognito, but the concierge and the maître d' in the French Room pretend to know who he is: a writer of some sort. Poet, playwright, novelist, it's an honor to have you with us, sir. The Great Man is embarrassed by flattery and pretends not to understand. He has had three or four drinks at lunch but is fully sober. And what is this music wafting through the busy lobby? And can it be a real harp played by a real woman placed there unobtrusively between two fat gilt columns close by the elevators? The Great Man approaches with head bowed, tears pleasantly stinging his eyes. It might be said that the young woman harpist reminds him of his daughter, long estranged. Or of his first love, long forgotten. For nearly an hour he stands behind one of the pillars listening to the harpist playing Debussy, Ravel, Schubert, sweet waterfall renditions of Beethoven and Liszt. He is the only person in the lobby who appears to be listening, but the harpist plays bravely, with sporadic swirls of gusto. Her long delicate fingers plucking the strings, fingertips quick and deft, and he isn't going to fall in love with her. She is young: younger than his daughter. Decades younger than his wife. A beautiful face, if rather narrow at the brow. Silvery hair falling straight and lank past her thin shoulders; that silvery pale skin that wears out soon. She wears bridal white silk, long skirt, long puckered sleeves, white silk shoes with a very high heel. The Great Man considers tipping her, then decides against it: she is an artist, like him, and would be insulted. The Great Man is not visibly weeping. The Great Man knows not where he is, or why.

In *The Cloud of Unknowing* it is told us we must "crush all knowledge and experience of all forms of created things and of yourself above all. . . ." The Great Man owes his greatness to such stratagems of the soul.

The Great Man is being driven to his next appointment in an immense black gleaming limousine. Sporty as a hearse, with a bar in the rear quarters. A small TV set, a uniformed Hispanic driver, young and handsome. The Great Man has shaved and showered and has hidden his body inside a custom-made pinstripe flannel suit. His expensive shoes gleam, his ascot tie obscures his wattled throat. You fraud, whispers the Great Man's wife. How has it come to this? Fraud! Impersonator! The Great Man is not offended because the woman is unwell. He glances through his notes, his hands are not trembling, today is a day like any other. "You have never known me," he whispers. "None of you," he whispers. The handsome young Hispanic driver regards him in the rearview mirror. "Not a one of you," The Great Man whispers. He checks the little bar, but the decanters are empty, each and every one.

• • •

The Great Man dreams of a watery grave. He is trying to bail water out of the grave with his bare hands. Momma, he whispers. Oh Papa! Why did you abandon me! In the dream his wife is dead and he is lying or, to be precise, squatting, beside her, lungs filling with filthy water. He tries to bail water out of the grave, but it runs through his fingers. And more rain continues to fall, turning to mud around his haunches. When he wakes it is to a telephone ringing in a place he doesn't know, but then he realizes that in his grave he is dreaming of a telephone ringing in a place he doesn't know (a luxury hotel room, it seems—ventilator quietly humming all the night long), and his despair is such that he gives up trying to save himself, he falls back into the watery filth beside a corpse said to be his wife, his wife who loves him and whom he loves, it's an old story chiseled in granite at their heads.

Many hands clapping, but their sound is muted, as if undersea. The Great Man cannot hear quite so well as he did when he was young. He cannot see quite so well as he did when he was young. There are other things he cannot do quite so well as he did when he was young, but he does not care to think of them now that he is the Great Man. In any case he considers it a fair trade—as he tells the roomful of journalists—to have lost his youth and vigor and to have gained greatness. He would not have done it any other way. He would not have done it any other way. Not done any other way, thank you, and what is the next question?

The Great Man is lonely amid so many well-wishers, so on the third day of his visit he slips away to visit the famous "fish round" at the aquarium. In this exhibit the human spectator stands at the center of a large glassed-in ring in which sea bass, sea trout, bluefish, and grouper fish of all sizes swim. The fish swim around the human spectator without taking notice of him, concentrated on their swimming. In the ring a gentle ocean current is simulated—one knot an hour. The fish swim against this current. Ceaselessly. All in the same direction. All at the same approximate speed. How placid, thinks the Great Man, who is beginning to get frightened. How idyllic, thinks the Great Man, who is beginning to feel ill. He turns slowly on his heel, watching sea bass, sea trout, bluefish, and grouper fish of all sizes swim behind their glass wall oblivious of his presence. . . . Perhaps he is not there at all? When the Great Man fails to return to his limousine at the appointed time the young Hispanic driver comes to fetch him. And where is he but at the center of the famous "fish round," turning slowly, slowly on his heel, eyes wet with tears of recognition and terror.

The Great Man is expected to eat in public. An immense throng of admirers. Faces, teeth, smiles. He cleans his glasses and frowns at his hands, to glance up is to confront the void. He cleans his glasses for several protracted minutes. "Thank you," he says. "I have been told that you are my immortality." The Great Man is placed at a table facing out into the void. Many circular tables, many smiling guests. Strangers, are they? Or is that his son, newly dead, seated at a table at the rear, arms folded across his chest? A predominance of women, as always. Women! The bearers of culture no less than of children, one would think they'd get weary finally, stand staring as it all rushes down the drain swirling and being sucked down the drain in a counterclockwise motion, make no effort to halt it. The Great Man must conjure up his soul, it's been misplaced. He tries to eat, with little visible success—the bright green slice of kiwi fruit on his plate hurts his eyes. Several glasses of red wine in rapid succession and then he's given no more. Who are these people? don't ask. Why are we here in this cavernous room together? don't ask. What is this food I must eat for the nourishment of my body? don't ask. The Great Man bows his head as if in prayer or mortification. The Great Man isn't dozing off, is he. The Great Man is roused to be presented with an award, which it appears he has forgotten he is to receive. "Thank you," he says. Smiling his nipped-in cagey smile. Fixing his vision to the horizon, where faces are effaced. How simple life. At such moments. Applause, applause. Applause like oxygen titillating the brain. "Thank you," murmurs the Great Man. "I have been told you are my immortality"—a shy whisper.

•   •   •

The Great Man has been married to the same woman for a very long time. He has betrayed her often, with numerous women. The Great Man cannot be held responsible because, as a Great Man, he is placed in temptation's way a good deal more than the rest of us.

In his hotel room the Great Man discovers a large basket of fruit and a bottle of French champagne awaiting him. Compliments of the management. Welcome. The cellophane rattles so loudly as he undoes the wrapping that the Great Man cannot proceed.

Once the Great Man waited in a hotel room for a telephone call that did not come. From his estranged son. And eventually the call did come, in another hotel room. Hello, Father? the boy shouted across the miles. Hello? Hello? The connection was poor. The boy wanted money. The boy never had a chance, it was said. Never got started, it was said. Living all his life in *his* shadow. (Meaning the Great Man's shadow, which is immense.) Hello, Father, you old fart Father, I want money, Father, sure I'll pay it back, Father, you old bastard Father, you know I adore you. The boy is now aged and dying, or dead. The Great Man remembers standing beside a hospital bed tightly clasping his wife's hand. Protocol suggests that you do not remark upon, or even take note of, the thin smell of vomit at such times. Acute liver disease, kidney failure, coppery-bright skin, eyes puffed shut. The usual. No stigma attached—alcoholism *is* a disease. The boy never had a chance, the Great Man is told. But don't blame yourself. Forty years old, the heart and liver and kidneys of an eighty-year-old, but don't blame yourself.

The Great Man says coldly, I won't. Brushing his snowy hair back from his noble forehead, eyes affixed to eyes in the usual mirror stare. Crush all knowledge of created things and of yourself above all and so on and so forth, amen. I won't. Don't worry, I won't.

The Great Man was unfaithful to his wife in the old days so frequently it came to seem to him that his wife must have known. Yes, but I love you best. Yes, but I love *you*. No, I don't know why. Why? I don't know why. In the cocktail lounge of the luxury hotel the Great Man sits contemplating such things. A man's character is revealed at such moments. The Great Man has been married a very long time. He loves his wife. He recalls the night a mad girl rang their doorbell saying she was in love with him, she was lovesick for him, would he not take her in? and the Great Man had hidden away until his wife fetched him saying it was all right. She'd opened a door, light fell inward in a crescent. In a neutral voice she said, You can come out now, it's all right, she has gone away to drown herself, it's all right. Yes, but I love you best. Yes, but I don't know why. Yes, I will never do it again, I am aging, I am gaining in wisdom. Why? I don't know why. Why?

The Great Man's last mistress—we are talking nostalgically of years, years ago—was in the habit of wearing Chinese brocade jackets, long dresses, long scarves and veils. Jade green flashing eyes were her primary feature, and she used them to great effect. She was a poet, an actress. She lived life to the fullest. The Great Man, no longer young, was flattered by her pursuit of him, though he was told she had boasted beforehand that she would seduce the Great Man and afterward tell tales of him, braided into her verse. This would indeed happen, eventually. But not until the Great Man's death.

The Great Man telephones his wife. I am so lonely. Please forgive me. Do you forgive me? I am so lonely. I love you. Why is your voice so distant? Hello? Hello?—holding the telephone receiver between his chin and shoulder while he selects grapes out of the fruit basket, plump juicy purple Concord grapes. Hello? Hello? Popping them one by one into his mouth and bursting them against his palate, then spitting the seeds into a paper napkin balled in his fist. Hello? Are you there?

From the backseat of the limousine the Great Man contemplates his driver. A glass partition separates them at all times. The young man is perhaps thirty. Of Hispanic descent and handsome: sleek black oiled hair, olive-dark skin, very dark eyes. He wears a dark coat, a striped shirt, an ordinary necktie, an inexpensive wristwatch, slightly oversize, on his left wrist. Don't you know who I am? the Great Man thinks in honest bewilderment. The young man drives with studied efficiency, makes no extravagant gestures, is polite to his distinguished passenger but shows not the slightest sign of curiosity. Hence the Great Man himself responds with dignity. No intemperate tips, no cheery nervous small talk, what is your name? how old are you? are you married? are you happy? what is the substance of your life? do you know who I am? don't you care who I am? what can I do to make you care, you arrogant little bastard? You fall in love eventually with your hired drivers, the Great Man was warned, by a fellow Great Man, winner of the Nobel Prize a few years back. Otherwise it is unbearable!—unbearable.

The Great Man is moderately disappointed at first, but only at first, seeing in the overhead light how the harpist's skin is rather coarse, how thin and lank her silvery hair. But her eyes are bright and not merely with drink! She's highly charged, eager to talk. *She* knows who the Great Man is. Sure I'm lonely, she says, swallowing down a mouthful of champagne, who wouldn't be lonely in this city if you're from out of town like I am at first I seriously doubted I could play the harp like this in a place like this but I need the money to be frank and, well—I need the money. Anyway I just play music I love and if anyone stops to listen I'm grateful. I have no pretensions these days. I have some ambition sure but I have no pretensions, I know I'm a damned good harpist but there aren't, you know, enough slots for us all—openings with orchestras. It's who you know, too. It's politics. You understand? Maybe I'm not the best harpist in the world but I'm a damned good harpist and they don't grow on trees. *You*, you don't have to think of such things but I do, that's one of the differences between us. Her voice is low and whining as his daughter's had been aged fifteen, sixteen, those terrible years. She is older than the Great Man anticipated but that isn't important. Just a friendly drink in his hotel room in the privacy of his hotel room a friendly drink or two and maybe something to eat later on if she's hungry if the Great Man can face food. What I'd like, dear girl, is to hire you for the evening—that is (with a quick gentle smile, a lowering of his eyes) hire you and your harp, and be privately entertained: Debussy, Ravel, Schubert, all the rest! Sorry, says Gwen with a look of genuine regret, I don't think that's possible. The Great Man offers fifty dollars an hour? one hundred dollars an hour? but sorry, says Gwen, blushing, that really *isn't* possible. The management wouldn't, you know, like it a whole lot. Then what is possible? asks the Great Man with his nipped-in plaintive smile. The harpist is taller than he by an inch or two but no matter. His own daughter is taller than he if he recalls correctly. No matter. Champagne, strawberries, mints wrapped in gold foil, compliments of the hotel. Gwen is my name, Gwendolyn's too long I suppose, she has small watchful eyes pale lashes and colorless eyebrows, prim and gawky and girlish and overexcited, her dress fits her loosely in the bust and is old-fashioned without being charming, sleeves a bit soiled at the cuffs and elbows, raw silk's beautiful, though, draw your fingertips across it, a raised pattern in the fabric and covered buttons a cascade of them down the front, fifteen? twenty? tiny buttons and high-heeled shoes slightly soiled at the toe which Gwen kicks off sighing lying back on the sofa opening her eyes wide. This place! says Gwen. Christ! Isn't it something!—two hundred dollars a night for this room, isn't it, who the hell can afford such prices but I'm not jealous after all they're paying my salary, Gwen says pleasantly high within minutes and laughing loudly as the Great Man laughs surprised and worried suddenly wanting this woman gone for what if his wife telephones? what if she pays a surprise visit to the hotel?—a trick she has not done for twenty years but you can't predict. But Gwen won't budge. High shrill thrilled laughter, gums showing pink and aggressive, the Great Man wants to be alone in this room wherever this is to gaze out the window at the overcast sky and think his melancholy thoughts of mortality and time's passing and the rest but soon he's out of breath laughing and by Christ he *likes* women even gawky girlish women he *likes* them what's the sin in that? Startling them with his attention, suddenly fierce with passion and eloquence, flattering, pleading, pleasing, what you lose in vigor you gain in technique as in art for isn't that the primary law of art? of life? A fair trade, the Great Man insists. And what is the alternative? The bitch plays coy but he's gentle (biographers take note) actually

rather shy, uncertain (biographers take note) stroking the woman's
hands caressing the fingertips from which such beautiful music
springs asking questions everyone asks of harpists, Don't the strings
hurt? don't your fingertips get raw? and Gwen drains her glass with
her free hand and shrugs, saying, Well—something has to hurt, or
nothing happens. So the Great Man kisses her fingertips. Does this
come next? He kisses her hands, back and front. Her wrists—those
delicate blue arteries. And next? Tears welling up in his eyes, his
wise old eyes that have gazed upon so much, O love don't deny me,
that kick in the gut he never quite expects but there it is, sobbing,
an old man sobbing, Oh, please have mercy will you have mercy?
The harpist stiffens as they all do, then relents melts as they all do,
it is a simple matter to be kind to the Great Man and perhaps he will
remember you in his will? Silvery hair pleasantly disheveled and a
whiff of female flesh a bit overheated, small shrewd eyes shining.
When did you first begin to take harp lessons, when did you know
the harp was to be your destiny? You are so beautiful. Do you know
how beautiful you are? lipstick eaten partly off her lower lip, she's
been chewing at her lower lip and now yes, may I use the bathroom?—and afterward she will say coquettishly, You're married,
aren't you? and he will say, It's a complicated tale too complicated
to tell, and Gwen if Gwen is her name will say, yawning sadly, I
was once married, too, or maybe she will say a bit defiantly, *I* have
never been married, a downturn of her mouth showing she isn't
bitter though perhaps a bit disappointed (she is thirty-four years old,
she suddenly confides) but then, well! she has her music after all.
That *tickles*, she says, giggling loudly and the waiter wheels the cart
into the room discreet and murmurous yes sir, no sir, *thank* you sir
with a flash of dark Hispanic eyes. They dine lavishly if carelessly
on country pâté and French bread, Russian caviar on the menu at
twenty-eight dollars a shot, a good Beaujolais, vintage 1976, no
matter the bill—the Great Man's way is paid by others. Old fraud,
whispers his wife. Just look at you! Old fart, whispers his dying son.
You're a real *character*, exclaims the harpist, wriggling her bare toes
and fixing him with a look of passion. The Great Man kisses her
knees, her belly, burrows his face between her legs, bluefish sea bass
grouper fish of all sizes swimming around and around in the same

direction, the ocean's current gently mimicked, the ocean's awful silence. Now and then, he'd noticed, one of the fish would fall behind, turn dazed and vague to the side, lose the rhythm of the swim and what fate awaits? don't ask. I love you, the Great Man declares, sobbing in gratitude and relief, old heart thumping in his chest. And I love you, someone replies, teasing and pinching his cheek. She only wants to break his heart!

The Great Man is driven to the airport, his hosts bid him farewell, many hands are shaken, autographs signed. The Hispanic driver has been replaced by a plump perspiring uniformed chauffeur who smiles in a craven fashion the Great Man ignores. He'd vomited up more than he'd eaten or drunk so there's a kind of virtue in that. Makes you feel innocent, virginal. Crush all knowledge of forms of created things and of yourself above all heaving up your guts in the toilet then rinsing your mouth afterward eyes locking into eyes in the mirror. Now first-class accommodations and the stewardess adjusts his seat, like this, sir, will you have a champagne cocktail, sir, he licks his lips declining with infinite regret and the great heart of the plane is revved up mimicking his own and an hour later flying eastward into the sun the Great Man wakes from his doze to hear the plane's engines falter and to see fire streaking from the plane's silvery wings, it is now! it will happen now! at last! already his fellow passengers are screaming the stewardesses stumble and plunge in the aisle the pilot's voice is raised over the loud-speaker but no one hears since within a matter of seconds the plane seems to be veering sideways slicing the air passengers and crew will be utterly lost but the Great Man wakes in time his heart thumping in his chest his cheeks hotly wet with tears. Please forgive me, he will beg of that nice brunette stewardess who offered him a drink, please don't speak ill of me, do you know who I am?

The Heir

Speak to me only of people who are dying, in pain, he said. Or
already dead. Speak of things vanishing, or rotting, giving off a
stink, he said. But when I drew breath to speak he interrupted at
once saying that I was blocking the light from the window. So I
moved to another chair close by his bed. He then complained that
I was sucking up all his oxygen and how could he compete with a
brute like me in his weakened state, his lungs all shot to hell?—so
I moved the chair to the foot of the bed. He then complained that
I was staring at him as at a coffined corpse at a wake. And did I
know I'd grown immense, my face bloated? My mouth, he said, was
a greedy little suction cup. My eyes, he said, were bright and hard
and empty as glass marbles, revealing each of my thoughts and each
was more loathsome than the one preceding. Didn't I know he
could read my mind? he asked, laughing his barking-wheezing laugh
that brings up the coin-size clots of phlegm, and sometimes blood.
Transparent as a giant jellyfish, I was, and with the appetite of one.
My heartbeat was liquid and pulpy, the sloshing contracting peri-
stalsis of my stomach was disgusting to one in his ethereal state and
would I please get out? but when I rose to leave he repented, and,
taking hold of my wrist in his fingers, which were thin and chill as
bare bones, said, Where are you going? are you afraid of me? don't
you love me? would you abandon me to this place? So I sat again,
in the first chair by the window, blocking the light until the light
ran out.

"Shot"

Loneliness sharpens the senses. In this new place where her parents had come to work the girl slept poorly and woke each morning at dawn, or before dawn, to a strange noise in the near distance—shouting, or loud singing, or a dog's repetitive hysterical barking. She lay in bed without moving or breathing and without thinking, listening to the sound with its serrated edges, the texture of mica-studded rusty earth, yet there was something moist and eager about it too, a shameless percussive rhythm that could belong to no machine, only to life. The sound called to her, tugged at her bowels. She dreaded it entering her sleep.

Gradually, with morning, other noises intervened. Diesel trucks on the highway bounding the suburban subdivision to the east, construction crews engaged in building new homes close by, bulldozers, chain saws, garbage trucks, jet bombers from the Joshua Tree Air Force Base at the edge of the desert. In the girl's own household there was likely to be uninterrupted quiet since neither her mother nor her father believed in television or radio news or inconsequential chatter in the crucial hour before they left for work but when, the single time the girl inquired of them if they'd heard that strange noise, "off in the distance, like someone calling for help," the noise had faded or ceased or been drowned out by other noises, so her mother said, after listening, or seeming to listen, for perhaps five seconds, that she couldn't hear anything out of the

ordinary, and her father, annoyed by the question, but making an
effort to be polite, merely smiled, and shook his head no, not having
made much of an effort to listen at all. As always his thoughts were
elsewhere where no one, not even his wife, was encouraged to
follow.

One morning in midsummer when the family had been living in
the new house for about a month and the girl was again wakened
by the strange sound she decided to track it to its source. Barefoot,
in her pajamas, she went downstairs, and stood on the bare concrete
terrace at the rear of the house, listening intently, and fixing the
sound at approximately eleven o'clock in terms of her position. It
could not have been more than a mile away, probably less. That was
to the northeast, for the sky was reddening there, quickened with
light like an opening eye beyond the dun-colored foothills of the San
Bernardino Mountains. This morning the sound was a harsh careless sobbing that grated against the girl's nerves. She thought, I
don't really want to know what it is!

Her parents left for work at eight o'clock: though they were not
assigned to the same project they worked in the same complex of
government buildings known locally as the Institute, and they
drove together in the same car. Shortly afterward the girl bicycled
out of the subdivision, along the coyly curving asphalt drives past
stucco ranch houses with Spanish-style roofs and grassless lawns
seemingly held in place by spindly trees and shrubs, houses virtually identical with the one the girl's father had bought for them
except in color, the positioning of the garage, and the degree of
newness and rawness, and as she approached the highway where,
now, the diesel trucks were in full force, she could hear the sound
only intermittently, like a radio station fading, and returning, and
fading again, but she knew she was going in the right direction.

She left San Jacinto Estates and after a little difficulty crossed the
busy highway and pedaled for about a quarter mile along the shoulder until she came to an unpaved road where instinct told her to
turn: she hadn't heard the sound for a few minutes but guessed it
might be coming from this direction. To her left was a deep irriga-
tion ditch in which, as if grudgingly, brackish water glinted; to her
right were shabby little bungalows and tar-paper shanties, places at

which it seemed rude to stare, debris strewn about the burnt-out yards, hulks of old automobiles and pickup trucks in fields, small children playing in the dirt oblivious of her passing. It was early but the desert-dry air was warming minute by minute. Unlike the light to which the girl had been accustomed, three thousand miles to the east, filtered and softened by pollutants in the air, this light seemed to emanate whitish and glaring from all directions; it rose from the mineral-glinting earth to strike sparks in her eyes. The girl knew that the world through which she moved was composed of structural fictions—ideograms of a kind, her father would have said—for where she saw light, color, texture, solid shapes, where indeed she felt the physicality of solid shapes, and experienced herself as one, there existed nothing but a cascade of ever-shifting and -changing atoms and molecules, substanceless as hieroglyphics on a computer screen, in some mysterious way linked to the rhythms of the human brain; yet, for all her knowing, for all her having been trained to know, she did not somehow believe. You reach out to touch a phantasmal world and your hand goes right through it—*except your hand does not go through it.* That was the small stubborn fact only a baby could utter and the girl, no longer a baby, no longer dared utter it.

Now the sound resumed and the girl heard it for what it was, distinctly: a dog's barking.

A dog's barking!—so commonplace after all.

But there was a special urgency to it. A sound as of words in a nightmare scramble. Where you hear, but can't understand—you understand but you don't *know.*

The girl bicycled to the dead end of the road, drawn by the dog. And there, in the front yard of a clapboard bungalow, in a mean grassless space littered with human debris and dog feces, a dog that might have been a German shepherd, or a husky, or a mixture of each, was tied by a chain leash to a stake: straining at the leash and barking frantically at the girl who had come to stare at him. So this was it! This! The dog was thick-bodied, ungainly, clearly old; with silver-tipped fur covered in dust and grime; wild rheumy-red eyes, a slavering muzzle, sharp yellowed teeth bared in a ferocious grin. He had been a handsome dog once but now suffered from a bad case of the mange, especially around his ears, and there was something raw and red and terrible about his neck. The iron stake to which his chain was affixed had been driven into the ground beside the bungalow's semirotted front stoop, and in the desperate radius of this ten feet the dog had worn the earth into grooves and ruts with his toenails. There was the evidence here of numberless weeks of captivity by night and by day.

"Nice dog! Good dog! Nobody's going to hurt you!" the girl called out weakly. In truth she was frightened that the dog would tear himself loose from his chain and attack her. No more than fifteen feet separated them and there appeared to be no one home in the bungalow—no car in the rutted driveway, no face at any of the windows.

A phrase of the girl's father's came to mind—*The intersection of certain sets is surely empty.*

The girl stared; the dog barked. Where at a distance the barking had had an almost mechanical sound, up close it seemed alive, as sound, twisting and writhing invisibly in the air, wave upon wave of furious indecipherable speech washing against the girl; buffeting her, rocking her with its violence. An immolation of sheer light and noise was about to explode in her brain but the girl could not break away—stood hunched, straddling her bicycle, hands pressed over her ears.

She had traced the mystery to its source but, at its source, the mystery had deepened. Why would a dog's owners, who presumably loved him, or in any case wished him well, tie him up so brutally, and go away, and forget him?—leave him to his animal misery? Did he bark with such fury for hours of the day? With so little provocation? And the neighbors didn't hear, or didn't care, or were reluctant to complain? In the residential neighborhoods the girl knew city police would be called at once if a dog barked this loudly and continuously; in particular, the girl's parents could not have borne it. But a grove of shabby palm trees separated this bungalow from the bungalow next door and maybe, in such a neighborhood, that was sufficient; maybe nobody did hear. In the wide radius of those presumably within earshot—and there must have been many—the girl might have been the only person who heard.

What did it mean, the girl wondered—that a living creature, animal or human, should make such sounds? and that no one cared enough to interfere?

The little one-story house in which the dog's owner or owners lived had been worn to a gray, neutral, weather-ravaged shade. Blinds had been drawn over its windows, some of its clapboards were hanging loose. It was shabby but not one of the shabbier dwellings on the road. The yard was littered with trash, especially in back, as if it were a dumping ground—cartons, food packages, bottles, tin cans—particularly beer cans—but there were several new-looking brightly striped canvas lawn chairs in the shade of the palm trees and a portable aluminum barbecue as splendid as any in San Jacinto Estates.

As if exhausted the dog lay down suddenly in the dirt. He was panting hard; he continued to bark in brief coughlike spasms, but less excitedly; it must have been impressed upon his consciousness, however dim and suspicious, that the girl was no threat. "Nice dog!" she called out, heartened. He *was* an old dog, and clearly in poor health. His long loose wet tongue lolled, dripping saliva; his shoulder and back muscles rippled beneath his coarse, matted fur; his scabby ears were in constant agitation from flies circling his head. There were flies too around the plastic dishes set out for him and in hazy glittering clouds around the feces scattered in the yard—some of the feces dried and desiccated, others fresh. The girl sniffed the air and her face crinkled.

The dog gave a heaving little shudder, stretching out his forelegs as if settling in for sleep, lowering his head, and the girl saw to her horror that the chain had been fastened directly—and tightly—around the dog's neck, not attached to a collar; and that the fur there was eaten away. It looked almost as if the chain had grown into the dog's flesh. . . . There were scabs, ugly-looking wounds, the glisten of fresh blood.

The girl looked quickly away as if she had seen something forbidden but the shock of it ran through her like an electrical charge.

"Hey there—hel*lo!* You looking for me?"

A woman in a housedress had opened the screen door at the side of the bungalow and was leaning out, blinking in the sunshine like a nocturnal animal. Her skin looked white and moist as bread dough and the housedress was wrapped so loosely around her, tied with a sash, that her pale thighs showed, and the shadowy crevice between her breasts. She was staring at the girl and both frowning and smiling. She might have been any age from thirty to fifty.

"You looking for me?" she repeated.

"No," said the girl shyly. "I just—"

"You live up the road, huh? But I don't guess I know your name?"

The girl stood straddling her bicycle, smiling in confusion. She wanted badly to escape but feared it would seem rude, with the woman looking so intently at her, and now smiling, as if they were indeed neighbors. And there was the dog.

"You live up the road? Where d'you live?" the woman asked, stepping outside. She was attractive, with long untidy glistening black hair like an Indian's or a Mexican's; her face shone as if it had been scrubbed with steel wool and her eyes too shone, with an unnatural, alert brightness, like chunks of charcoal embedded in her white face. "What's your name?"

"Donna."

"Oh yes? Donna, is it? Did I maybe know that?"

The girl continued to smile, perplexed. "Donna" was the name of a girlfriend of hers, back east. "I don't know," she said.

"I see you and Shot have been making friends," the woman said. "That's nice." In the direct sunshine it looked as if an older, finely wrinkled face had been pressed atop a young, harshly good-looking face like that of a Hollywood actress of the old days. She smiled repeatedly, strangely, with an elastic sort of enthusiasm. "C'mon closer, Donna! You can pet him. Pet poor Shot."

"Oh—is that his name? 'Shot'?" the girl asked.

The woman picked her way barefoot—her stubby-toed feet were very white, like her face—through the dog droppings and broken glass and pebbles, and squatted dramatically beside the dog, hugging him suddenly with feeling and crooning to him. The dog yipped and whimpered with pleasure and licked her hands and face with his tongue; his body quivered with joy. His long dirt-encrusted tail thumped against the packed earth. The girl stared and felt a small stab of envy. She asked again, "His name is 'Shot'?"

"*Buck*shot!" The woman laughed. "My husband's weird idea. But—it got shortened."

"What kind of a dog is he? A German shepherd?"

"He sure ain't a cocker spaniel or one of them little tiny weiner dogs, are you, Shot?" The woman clumsily straddled the dog's back, hugging him around the neck and playing at riding him. "Giddyup, Shot! Hey! Giddyup!" She was in a mood bright and electric and wayward such as the girl had never witnessed in an adult. "Want to pet Shot, Donna? Want to *ride* him? He won't bite, I promise."

"Oh, I don't think so," the girl said, smiling uncertainly.

"He won't bite—he's crazy about kids. Just give him a little pet on the head." The woman rubbed the dog's skull rather brusquely with her knuckles. He whimpered and thrashed about with pleasure. "C'*mon!*"

Summoned thus, the girl had no choice but to obey. She laid her bicycle down carefully in the driveway and approached the woman and the dog and reached out shyly to touch the dog's alert, quivering, high-held head. Did she hear growling?—a sound as of tiny pebbles grating deep in the dog's throat? "Shot, be *good*," the woman scolded. "Donna's a neighbor from up the road. She's a friend!"

The dog's fur was coarser than the girl would have imagined, like wire beneath her fingertips; and without warmth. The raw strip like a necklace around the dog's neck glistened with fresh blood. The girl felt slightly ill, seeing it. She did not understand why the woman took no notice. She said, "His neck—it's hurt?"

The woman said, "Oh—that's nothing. That's 'cause he's a bad boy pulling at his leash all the time." She kissed the dog's nose with a bit of fuss and got to her feet, swaying. A close stale powdery odor wafted from her. Through the opening of the rayon housedress the girl could see, without wishing to see, one of the woman's loose heavy vein-riddled breasts.

The girl said uncertainly, "It must hurt him, though—where it's bleeding? He might get blood poisoning, or gangrene?"

"Naw!" the woman said contemptuously.

The dog was staring up alertly at the girl, his lips drawn back from his yellow teeth. He barked loudly once, twice, then made a whimpering noise and busily licked the girl's fingers. Never in her life had a dog licked her fingers: how wet, how loose and soft, like a chamois cloth, that tongue! It was a shock too to see, close up, the dog's eyes. They were reddened and filmed over with moisture, there were clots of mucus in the corners, but, still, they were beautiful eyes—you could see it, up close. Brimming with passion, with something like thinking, yearning, willing.

The girl said, "But it must hurt him, around the neck there. He must feel pain."

"Naw, dogs don't feel pain," the woman said. Then laughed, relenting, "Or if they do they don't *say*."

The girl swallowed hard and persisted. "You keep him tied up all the time too I guess and he's lonely and barks and—"

"You wouldn't be the party up the road who's trying to make trouble for us, would you?" the woman asked pleasantly.

"Oh no," the girl said. "Actually I don't live—"

"Threatening to call the police and like that? The SPC fucking A?"

"Oh no."

"Look: this dog is my heart," the woman said feelingly, as if there might be some doubt. "When my husband left the last thing he said was, 'You keep Shot for protection,' and I said, 'Protection from what?' and he said, 'Protection from me.' " She laughed loudly and squeezed the girl's hand as if urging her to laugh, too. "You have to hand it to the sons of bitches—men! They always get the last word."

The girl smiled, embarrassed. She could think of no reply.

"You're maybe the daughter of those people?" the woman asked, peering into the girl's face. She was still squeezing the girl's hand and showed no inclination to release it.

"What people?"

"You know."

"What—what people?"

The woman continued to peer into the girl's face, for a long unnerving moment. Her eyes were very black and shiny but appeared to have no pupil; nor had she lashes, or eyebrows except for a thin stubbly arch—it looked as if she'd plucked them out. Excitement like phosphoresence played about her damp fleshy lips. "A person has got to have her dignity. If you take away a person's dignity you know what you got left? A pile of shit."

The girl tugged discreetly at her hand but the woman did not release it.

"Telling other people what to do—that's dangerous," the woman said. She spoke now in surges, quickly, and then slowly, as if she were making an effort to hold herself back. "That's how you get your head blowed off, some places. Say I know I got some problems but I don't need nobody else to tell me about them. Say I know Shot barks a lot 'cause he's excitable and the kids in the neighborhood tease him, throwing stones and shit, and he's tied up like he is 'cause I work, I work weird hours, I'm a beautician by profession and the only work I can get is part-time around here 'cause this is where I fucking ended up 'cause I made a wrong decision I didn't know was a wrong decision at the time so what do you want me to do about it—cut my throat? He left and that isn't enough he takes the car and he says he's coming back and I'm asshole enough to believe him but in the meantime like you can see I don't have no car which means I have to take the fucking bus or get a ride with somebody and now the telephone's out too for back payments and there's these self-righteous fuckers like your mommy and daddy I guess who think I got money to throw around?—money to burn?— money grows on trees and I just reach up and pick it?—like taking Shot to the vet when I fucking need the vet *myself* and I can't afford it and there's these things I need from the drugstore I can't afford and before the phone went out I got these weird calls keeping me up half the night and somebody broke glass all out front here and stuck razor blades in the dirt so I'd walk on them barefoot like I'm so trusting like I am—" Her voice had been spiraling like a singer's and now she broke off, breathing hard, considering. Her eyes were narrowed in shrewdness. She was leaning so close to the girl that the girl could feel her warm moist panting breath and taste its rankness. "Like I said—Shot's my *heart*. He's all I *got*. He forgives me anything 'cause he loves me. He doesn't judge! If I gave the command you know what he'd do, you stupid little cunt? He'd tear out your throat."

The girl stood perfectly still. The dog, nudging at her knees, was alternately barking and whining, snarling and whimpering. His long tail thumped from side to side. The woman said slyly, "D'you know what that command is, Donna?"

The girl licked her cold lips. "No."

"Huh? *Don't* you?"

"No."

"D'you want me to tell you, then?" the woman asked. " 'Cause if I say it out loud—!"

Sick with fear the girl shut her eyes. She was trembling violently, thinking, This is a mistake—this can't be happening. How do I know that this is me? How do I know that this is—now?

"No," the girl whispered.

"Say what?"

"No, *please.*"

" 'No, *please'!* That's how it is, huh? Stupid little cunt butting your nose in other people's business!" With a little shove the woman released the girl; but the girl did not dare make a move to escape. The dog was nudging against their legs in a display of frantic energy; doing a little dance in the dirt. He yipped, he whined, short staccato barks burst from him like bronchial coughing. In dreamlike terror the girl felt his damp nose and slavering mouth against her bare knees, nudged into the crotch of her shorts. How passionately he sniffed, as if sniffing were eyesight, or a kind of speech. . . . The woman was saying, in derision, "Go on, little girl—*go.* Get the hell back home."

The girl backed away. Her knees nearly buckled beneath her. The dog sprang forward, almost knocking her over, standing urgently on his hind legs, barking, whimpering, seeming to plead with her to take him with her. Until finally the girl was safely out of the radius of his chain and free of him and the woman, hands on her thighs, looked her up and down in mean delight and said, "You know what? You're not even pretty. *You'll have to make your way somehow else.*"

·   ·   ·

She fled, she returned home.

And she did telephone the SPCA. And the local police.

And whether they came to the woman's house at the end of the dirt road and saved Shot from his misery, or made any difference at all in the dog's life, she didn't know; she kept her windows closed in the morning and kept her air-conditioning unit on. It was hot weather, in any case.

Often, she heard dogs barking. In the distance.

Any number of dogs. For the world was filled with barking dogs after all.

Letter, Lover

I had been living in the city, in my new life, only a week before the first of the letters arrived.

Miss I see you! This is to say—and here several words had been crossed vigorously out—*you cant hide.*

The message was written in green ink, in neatly printed block letters, on a sheet of lined tablet paper. There was no stamp on the envelope: just my name and street address. Whoever had sent it had shoved it through the slot of my mailbox amid a long row of mailboxes in the foyer of my apartment house.

I had opened the envelope going upstairs, ripping it with my thumbnail, eager to see who'd written to me, but when I read these words my heart kicked in my chest and for a moment I thought I might faint.

I looked behind me, I was so frightened.

I thought, *Oh it's a joke.*

The second letter came a week later, I recognized the envelope at once, in my mailbox with legitimate mail: my name and street address, no stamp. He lived in the apartment building, maybe. Or might be one of my co-workers who'd followed me home.

Girl with blond hair—*slut cant hide. I SEE YOU.* The sheet of paper was wrinkled, soiled. Included with it was a small swatch of cloth shot with iridescent gold threads, cheap fabric, soiled, too, seemingly bloodstained.

I began to wear my hair pinned up, and a scarf over it. I removed the fingernail polish from my fingernails and never wore any again.

• • •

Other letters came for me, with stamps. I skimmed their contents quickly and set them aside. It was the plain square white envelope I looked for, in my mailbox. *High heel shoes—only sluts—*and here words were crossed out—*Dont hide from me because I see through the window & the wall BLONDIE.* Included with the third letter was a snapshot of a young woman walking with her head lowered, a young woman wearing my blue raincoat, my white scarf on her head, walking on a street close by. I recognized the graffiti-scarred brick wall. I recognized the coat and the high-heeled shoes. You couldn't see who the young woman was, her face had been destroyed by an angry barrage of pinpricks. There were pinpricks too in her breasts and crotch.

I stopped wearing high-heeled shoes, I avoided that street, that particular block. There was no point in provoking him.

We know it's unwise and to no purpose, to provoke such people. I was having difficulty sleeping. I trusted no one.

I kept the blinds to all my windows drawn during the day, and always at night. Even in the early morning when my kitchen window was flooded with sunshine I kept that blind drawn, I knew he might be watching. No point in taking chances. That's what they would say, afterward.

I wondered if the letters were being sent to me by God's will, or just by accident.

I went to the building superintendent and told him about the letters but I hadn't any to show him, one by one I'd torn them up, threw them away, there was no evidence. Once, after the fourth or the fifth letter came, I picked up the telephone receiver to call the police, but my hand shook so badly I couldn't dial. I went to the police precinct station but when a policeman asked staring at me could he help me, what did I want, I backed away, I said, No, nothing, no thank you, and fled. *You are such a liar & tramp, I can read your thoughts. Im your friend.*

How are you? How are *you?* How is everybody? That's good to hear. Are you well? You sound as if you have a cold! What's it doing there?—it's raining here. It's snowing here. Oh yes I'm feeling

much better. The sun is shining here. Yes my job is going well. Yes
I couldn't be happier. Yes I'm making friends. Yes but you didn't
call for two weeks. Is it cold there? Is it snowing there? Is the sun
shining there? When are you coming home? Yes I have many
friends. Yes the sun is shining. And how are *you?*

I worked on the forty-fourth floor of a building that rose sixty
floors into the sky. The upper windows were sometimes opaque
with fog, sometimes the sun shone fiercely through them: this was
"weather." Below, on the street, there was a different "weather."

All the inhabitants of the town I'd come from, every person I had
ever known, could have been fitted into that building, all lost from
one another in that space. *I watch you & see your pride but that
wont help. You know what will help you—NOTHING.*

Once, reading one of the messages, I came to myself standing in
a corridor on the third floor of my apartment house instead of the
second floor where I lived. My eyes were flooded with tears of
shame and confusion. In the distance, a baby was crying. At first I
thought it was myself.

As the letters came, one by one in their plain square white
envelopes, I tore them up, letters and envelopes both, and threw
them away. A sickness like nausea rose in me and I worried I might
show the shame of it in my face.

Then, one day, searching for a pair of stockings, I discovered the
letters in one of my bureau drawers, five or six of them, or seven,
intact!—in their original envelopes, neatly folded and preserved. So
I saw that it was meant for me to keep them after all, despite my
disgust.

I thought, This is evidence. Should I ever be required to provide
evidence.

I thought, Of course I must move away.

How obvious: I must return home.

It was Christmas. The first letter had come in the early autumn,
and now strips of cheap glittering tinsel and colored Christmas
ornaments were strung about the foyer of the apartment house
when, unlocking my mailbox, I saw another of the plain square

white envelopes inside. This time I could not bear to touch it. I stood for some minutes, unmoving. My eyes spilled tears. A fellow tenant, unlocking his mailbox close by, noticed me, and asked politely, "Is something wrong, miss?"

I did not know this man's name but I knew his face for I'd been aware of him as a fellow tenant, as one is aware of an object hovering in the periphery of one's vision that might, or might not, advance; an object that might, or might not, possess its own identity and volition. I saw my trembling fingers snatch up the envelope and hand it to the man, I heard my voice thin as frayed cloth—"I can't open it!"

Hesitating only a fraction of an instant, the man took the envelope from me.

This man whose name I did not know was a few years older than I, yet still young, with a frowning face, a somber manner. I knew, or believed I knew, that he lived on the floor above me, and that he lived alone.

He turned the envelope in his fingers, examining it.

Then he opened it, and unfolded the sheet of tablet paper, and read the message, standing very still as he read, and silent. Out of the envelope there fell something, not a snapshot but a clipping, from a glossy magazine, perhaps, I was never to see this clipping but supposed it might have been a photograph of a woman modeling lingerie, the young man picked it up and crumpled it in his fingers to save me the embarrassment of seeing. I was saying, "I don't know who it is who sends me these things, he doesn't let me rest, he won't ever let me go, he wants to drive me away and I've been so happy here," words that tumbled out without my understanding where they might lead, words that surprised me with their vehemence and boldness, "I went to the building superintendent, I went to the police, nobody can stop him, nobody can help me. . . ."

The young man reread the letter, his cheeks visibly reddening. I could hear his outraged breath.

Then he lifted his eyes to my face, it was the first time we exchanged that look which we would, over the course of weeks, then months, exchange many times, and he frowned, and said, "I'll keep this: you don't want to see this," and I whispered, "Thank you," and he said, "No you don't want to see this, it isn't very nice," and he folded up both the letter and the envelope, thoughtfully, and put them away in an inside pocket of his coat.

My Madman

She has a certain local renown, so there's bound to be envy, jealousy, hostility behind her back, she'd be a fool to think otherwise but still she's taken by surprise one day when a youngish man, a stranger, smiles as if he knows her well and edges uncomfortably close to her and says in a low loving voice, "I'd like to slam you right here"—one hand shielding his jaw and the other, balled into a fist, threatening to punch it.

They are alone together in an elevator that is ascending to the eighth floor of the university library where volumes on philosophy and theology are kept and she stares at the young man as if she hasn't heard what he has said. *Has* she heard? He says again, pleasantly, making the same gesture with his fist, "I'd like to slam you right *here*."

"Why?" she asks.

"Because you're so smug," he says. The elevator has stopped, the door eases open, he slips away with a smile at her over his shoulder. "Because—you're who you are."

And she's left staring after him, so surprised she isn't even frightened. Has she really heard what it is she's heard?

"But who am I?" she wonders.

She doesn't get out on the eighth floor but rides the elevator back down to the first where she wanders aimlessly for some minutes wondering should she report the incident or should she simply forget it? . . . If she reports it there will be a minor fuss and people will invariably talk about her, embroider tales about her, there'll be a version in which she is raped in an elevator (of course) and another version in which she is defined as "hysterical" (of course) and after all there was no assault of any kind; scarcely any insult; no obscene language or gestures. It might even be argued by the mad young man (for surely he is mad?) that he was only being playful. He was only being truthful.

You're so smug, he'd said. You are who you are.

She decides not to report the incident. She decides to forget it.

Now she recalls having seen the young man around campus from time to time without ever quite looking at him: big-headed, slope-shouldered, sallow-skinned, with watery eyes and a perpetual ironic smirk, the look of an underground creature intimidated by daylight. He always wears an unironed white shirt whose sleeves are rolled up to his elbows, his trousers are invariably shapeless and stained, he's an older graduate student, perhaps, in his thirties, the bloom of youth long faded—too many sunless days in the library stacks, too many hours spent taking notes in fluorescent-lit interiors, a small lifetime spent trying to please his elders. Perhaps he is brilliant in someone's eyes? Perhaps he is no longer a student. Just living on the periphery of what's called the university community, nowhere else to go.

She knows the type. They recognize one another.

She continues to see him occasionally in the library, on campus, in town. Always alone. Always walking quickly. A bookbag slung over his shoulder, hair spiky and disheveled. At public lectures and free concerts he arrives early and sits in one of the front rows, always on the aisle: lanky legs crossed, foot wagging compulsively. Sometimes he holds his head rigidly erect, other times he slouches, droops, his head bent at a painful angle. He takes notes furiously in a small notebook, shielding the page with his shoulder. She sits where she can see him, keep him in view. My madman, she thinks, wondering why, since that day, he has never approached her again.

Well, she thinks, preparing to grow older—it will have to do.

Cuckold

For D. H.

That evening he arrived home at the apartment approximately thirty minutes earlier than usual but perhaps this fact isn't relevant.

He called her name but she wasn't in the living room.

He called her name but she wasn't in the kitchen.

He called her name but she wasn't in the bedroom.

He called her name but she wasn't in the study.

He called her name but she wasn't in the bathroom.

Calling her name, beginning now to be worried, unless he was frightened, he returned to the living room switching on all the lights and like a fool or a madman or a desperate husband he stooped to peer beneath the sofa though he knew she wouldn't be in such a place, he returned to the kitchen opening a closet door though he knew the gesture was both futile and demeaning, *Where are you?* he called, *where are you hiding?* switching on lights as he hurried from room to room and in the bathroom calling her name he heard an eerie echo as of the interior of a seashell held to a child's ear for the first time, and in the bedroom he knelt peering beneath the bed though of course she wouldn't be in such a place, he pleaded, he threatened, he called her name like an incantatory prayer awkwardly translated from a Middle Eastern tongue, he threw open the closet doors, he looked behind the bookshelves, in despair he left the apartment calling her name in the hall, he knocked on neighbors' doors but no one had seen her, his face now beet red, his pride in a puddle at his feet, he climbed the stairs to the roof but she wasn't on the roof, he took the elevator down eleven floors to the street but she wasn't on the street, he circled the block in the rain his heart beating like giant dice shaken violently in a cardboard cup but she wasn't there, he returned to his building and took the elevator back upstairs and let himself back in the apartment and when he stepped inside the living room there she was . . . there, restored to him . . . miraculously restored to him . . . sitting regarding him with her lovely ironic imperturbable eyes in whose pupils he was reflected an infinitesimal fraction of an inch tall, and he whispered, *Bitch! where have you been!* and knelt to feel her pads: were they damp, were they cold, were they gritty from the street. But he couldn't tell.

The Escape

W hen, those years, we returned home from school in the late afternoon it was frequently to discover that the door to our apartment was bolted on the inside, so that our key, our lone key shared by the four of us, was not sufficient to let us in. Shyly then we rapped on the door, rang the bell at first tentatively, then with increasing desperation, minutes would pass, we might retreat temporarily to sit on the stairs doing homework (though the corridor light was poor), then renew our effort in an hour, plaintive voices pitched low so that neighbors might not overhear and, guessing our predicament, take pity on us. "Mother—it's only us, please let us in—" we would beg until finally, and by now we were likely to be crying, altogether miserable in our navy blue woolen jumpers and starched white blouses we'd been wearing since seven-thirty that morning, there would come a fumbling at the lock, the strangely sullen sound of the bolt sliding free, and we would push the door open, not eagerly but cautiously, with regard for Mother's nerves. She would take a quick step or two back into the shadows as we entered the unlit vestibule, her eyes gleaming white, glancing behind us as if vigilant, even now, against an unannounced enemy; yet she stood tall, dignified, beautiful, head uplifted, a crocheted black shawl around her shoulders and her arms tightly crossed beneath her breasts, her thick splendid hair perfectly rolled up and back from her face, gleaming like ebony, fixed in place with large tortoiseshell and mother-of-pearl combs. Exclaim-

109

ing softly, half-chiding and half-affectionate, "You girls!—always mislaying your key!"

The door would be locked again, and bolted.

And gravely Mother would kiss us, one by one. Mother's marble-cool lips, pressed against our warm foreheads. One by one.

Those years, the nuns did their best to teach us such adult concepts as Justice. But we understood that Justice did not apply to children, let alone to us.

Sometimes in the night we would wake abruptly to the sound of sobbing.

Melodic, like the sea, rising and falling, muffled, then higher-pitched as if deliberate, a current of anger beneath.

A scent of bruised camellias filling the apartment, most concentrated in the shadows.

In our nightgowns, barefoot and shivering, we would creep quietly to Mother's bedroom at the far end of the corridor, hearing the sobbing more pronounced, interspersed perhaps with low soft exclamations, we dared to push in the door to discover Mother, not in bed (Mother's bed, large, high, with four brass posts and a dazzling white lace spread, would not even have been turned back), but seated in her chair by a window, fully clothed, head uplifted, a cigarette burning in her fingers. If there was a moon, moonlight would illuminate her heavy-lidded eyes, the glisten of tears on her cheeks, but when we asked, "Mother, why are you crying?" she would regard us calmly, baring her teeth in a perfect white smile, and say, "How silly you girls are tonight! I'm not crying."

Or, sighing, exhaling smoke in a languorous plume, "My God—*why* was I given daughters, and not sons!"

Or, the answer that most frightened us, since at such times Mother fixed her teary-bright gaze on us with a particular sort of satisfaction, enveloping the four of us in a single dilated gaze as if we were but one helpless creature, "One day, you won't have to ask."

Yet Mother never failed to kiss us, one by one. Those cold perfect lips, our feverish foreheads.

• • •

If you are beautiful you will be followed in the street—as Mother has been, and still is. ("And out of that insult, the litter of *you* sprang!")

But if you are not beautiful, no one will so much as glance at you.

Assuming of course that you are Female, and not Male.

Our suitcases were packed, a half dozen of them, waiting just inside the vestibule to the front entrance of the apartment building, but the taxi was late. Mother awaited us impatiently, smoking a cigarette. She wore her black belted raincoat and her hair was covered with a black silk scarf. As soon as we entered the building, wet and bedraggled from the rain, and blinking at the unexpected sight of Mother in the vestibule, she hugged us, relieved, yet annoyed— "You girls! The taxi might have been here by now, and where for God's sake were *you!*"

Mother's possessions were of uniformly high quality, and her matched luggage was no exception. These were leather suitcases, a deep burnished wine red, delicious to smell, yet each was badly battered and scratched, from years of ill usage. The eldest of us remembered, as if in a dream, having seen Mother stride purposefully to the staircase railing on our floor and drop one of the suitcases down the stairwell, to land with an alarmingly loud thud on the marble floor of the vestibule six stories below.

The taxi arrived—a striking vehicle, larger than an ordinary car, a gleaming black, with a front grill like a wide chrome smile. Mother spoke to the driver in an urgent whisper, as he carried the suitcases to the taxi, set them into the trunk and onto the rack affixed to the roof. As we climbed into the rear, in haste, stumbling over one another's feet, Mother said, as if thinking aloud, "This time—none of them know our plans. This time will be different."

The driver climbed into the front of the taxi, glanced at us curiously in the rearview mirror, and said, "Ma'am? Where shall I take you?"

Mother, half shielding her face with her gloved hand, said, with an air of nervous gaiety, "Oh—*you* know! We're making our escape!"

The driver's gnarled eyebrows met in a single line of perplexity over the bridge of his nose. "Ma'am? D'you mean the train station?"

Mother pressed a gloved finger over her lips. At such times she was both vehement and coquettish. "Just drive, sir, please!"

As the taxi swung away from the curb and we were thrown together, laughing breathlessly, gripping one another's hands, Mother said, in an undertone, "*This* time will be different, I promise!"

Our city was an old city, our neighborhood in the oldest district. Our street was one of worn cobblestones, wet, or wet-seeming, with a perpetual mineral glisten; like a riverbed at the bottom of steep canyon walls. At intersections, when the taxi was obliged to slow, or come to a stop, we could see how blocks of buildings dissolved into mist, or frank emptiness—not that the buildings were under construction, though in fact some were, but that they simply broke off, like jigsaw puzzles with parts missing. If Mother, smoking her cigarette, noticed, she gave no sign.

Traffic was dense on the main thoroughfares, at this hour of the day, thus our taxi moved slowly, in erratic surges of energy. Mother grew impatient, leaning forward to rap on the plastic partition that divided the front seat from the rear. "Driver? Why are you so slow? Don't you know a shorter route? Do you want us to miss our train?"

The driver regarded Mother in the rearview mirror with an expression of startled dismay. "Ma'am," he said, "nobody could get you there faster."

Mother persisted, "You have some purpose, do you? In slowing us down?"

"Ma'am?"

"You've driven us in the past, haven't you? My daughters and me?" Mother's voice rose, as if some invisible demon were pinching her. "You recognize our faces, do you?"

"Ma'am, I don't know what you're talking about!"

But Mother was aroused with purpose, resolution. Her pale cheeks were flushed and her normally hooded eyes shone. She cried, "They sent you, didn't they! Instead of the taxi I ordered they sent their own taxi, didn't they! *Let us out at once.*"

Useless for the taxi driver to protest, Mother never changed her

mind once she was set upon a course of action. So we found ourselves on the boulevard, in the midst of traffic, our half-dozen
suitcases carelessly deposited on the pavement, as Mother angrily
waved for another taxi. No one dared speak as Mother ventured out
into the street, risking injury, provoking drivers to sound their
horns, nor did we dare glance at one another for fear of seeing tears,
which are contagious.

Yet Mother succeeded in getting us another taxi, very like the
one we had abandoned, though driven by an older, brisk, gray-
haired man, wearing a visored cap, who brought us to the train
station within twenty minutes; but upset and irrevocably offended
Mother, whose nerves were so on edge, by smiling too familiarly at
her, and asking where she and her "pretty little girls" were going.
So this driver Mother refused to tip, on the grounds of insubordina-
tion and male buffoonery, handing over to him a dollar bill or two
and a good deal of loose change, exclaiming, "They have no *right*,
I will show them they have no *right*," and the driver blinked in
astonishment, began to protest, but thought better of it and hastily
retreated.

We had gamely taken up the suitcases, meaning to carry them
into the train station, the eldest of us determined to carry two
apiece (though the suitcases were strangely heavy, packed to bursting and strapped shut), but this Mother refused to allow, for we
might injure our internal organs, in any case it was a vulgar sight,
well-bred young girls grunting over luggage, thus a railway porter
had to be engaged, but this proved a difficult task not because there
were no porters on hand but because, perhaps on account of
Mother's attractive appearance, there were too many, converging
upon us, smiling and seeming solicitous, and Mother had to choose
among them, laughing nervously, both flattered and annoyed, for
such things were forever happening to her when she left the privacy
of our apartment, especially to risk escape from the city, and the
porters quarreled with one another, and Mother twice changed her
mind, engaging now one man, but now another, and in the confusion it suddenly came to light that one of the suitcases was
scratched—a thin but highly visible saw-toothed scratch, amid a
patina of older, less visible scratches. And naturally Mother protested, genuinely upset, and insisted upon speaking with the

station manager—"I won't be insulted, just because I am a woman
without a male companion!"

For the next ten or fifteen minutes we four stood at a discreet
distance from Mother, biting our lips and trying not to succumb to
anxious tears. When was our train scheduled to leave, we asked one
another, but none of us knew; nor did we dare speak to Mother for
fear of making things worse.

Finally, the matter of the scratched suitcase was resolved, and we
ventured into the chaos of the station, now pushing our luggage on
a porter's cart of our own, the four of us hurrying in Mother's wake.
We had no trouble following her tall, regal, striking figure amid the
crowd of strangers, though it seemed to us that the station had been
renovated and enlarged since our last visit, and even dimly familiar
landmarks, like the old domed kiosk at the center of the waiting
room, were gone. On all sides there was a dizzying turmoil of
motion, like water swirling rapidly as it is about to go down a drain;
ear-splitting train whistles; vendors' cries; unintelligible announce-
ments over the amplifying system; a din as of hundreds of barrels
rolling and echoing upward into the vaulted ceiling sixty feet overhead—a maze of open girders and elaborate nineteenth-century
metalwork where pigeons, swifts, and bats nested.

Seeking the ticket counter, which was not where it had been
previously, Mother had cautiously drawn her black silk scarf up to
hide the lower part of her face and turned up her raincoat collar.
Yet, still, she attracted attention, as much for her manner (both
shrinking and impetuous, fearful yet with an air of scarcely controlled desperation) as for her appearance. Men stared openly at her,
several politely inquired if she was in need of directions, but Mother
ignored them, as if unhearing, smiling brightly over her shoulder at
us and waving us on—"This way, girls! What slowpokes!"

At last Mother located the ticket counter, a marble ledge that
stretched literally out of sight in the gloom, now to find the correct
wicket, not so easy a task, thus more precious minutes were wasted
until Mother joined the end of a lengthy, slow-moving, sullen line
of travelers, and after forty-five frustrating minutes she found herself at the counter where, as luck would have it, poor Mother, the
clerk was an officious but supremely ignorant youngish man, or was
he in fact covertly rude, even mocking, misunderstanding Mother's

request for tickets at first, issuing her the wrong tickets, then insisting that the train she wanted no longer ran, all train service to that
part of the country had been discontinued, then reversing himself
saying no the train still ran but at irregular intervals—not at seven
thirty-five P.M., as Mother believed, but at seven thirty-five A.M.—
which was to say, not until morning.

Mother said hotly, "That's ridiculous. That's a lie."

The clerk pushed a timetable to Mother, who refused to touch it.
"Madame, see for yourself."

Mother wiped brusquely at her eyes with a handkerchief and
said, "It's just so *insulting*. That you lie to me so openly and so
crudely."

The clerk squinted at Mother with an expression of seemingly
genuine astonishment. "Madame? 'Lie'? I'm afraid I don't—"

Mother had removed her wallet from her handsome kidskin
handbag, to pay for the tickets, but suddenly, in the heat of the
moment, thrust it back into the handbag again, saying, "I've decided not to buy those tickets from you after all." Quickly, as the
clerk stared after her, she turned from the wicket, strode away,
signaling for us to follow, as naturally we did, disconcerted by
Mother's decision yet not truly surprised, for such abrupt reversals
had happened in the past.

It was not a propitious hour for our escape after all, as perhaps we
should have guessed.

"Come, girls! Hurry!"

Exhausted as we were, faint with hunger, we followed in
Mother's wake, pushing the cart high-piled with luggage, back
through the immense waiting room filled with strangers, back to
the entrance of the station, back to the confusion at the curb,
beneath the portico, where taxis were lined up awaiting passengers and where, in order to return home, we would have to engage
a taxi. Numbly but dutifully we followed, and unquestioningly,
as upon other, similar occasions, for it seemed self-evident that
our bodies were Mother's, and her body was ours, and that Death
might sweep all away, but never a part; so long as we remained
together, moving forward in one swift, fluid motion, we were safe,
we were inviolable.

• • •

"Quick! Get inside, and shut the door."

As soon as we scampered inside, Mother locked and bolted the door; threw herself breathlessly against it, arms outstretched. A single ferocious tear gleamed, like a gem, on her cheek.

It was now night, the numerous high-ceilinged rooms of the apartment cloaked in darkness.

As Mother pulled off her scarf, removed her coat to toss it across a chair, the four of us, still in our coats, tiptoed about switching on lamps, timidly reclaiming the rooms one by one. We saw that, in our absence, someone had been here—a pair of embroidered cushions were out of place on a sofa, a Chinese vase had been knocked from a mantel to shatter into pieces (these pieces we hastily swept up, and hid), drawers had been opened and carelessly shoved back. And though we had surely not been gone for more than three hours, the grandfather clock in the dining room had stopped; and petals had fallen, like clumps of heavy snow, from a bouquet of camellias fresh that very morning.

If Mother noticed these things she chose to say nothing.

"Well—we're home!"

Seeing that we'd lit her bedroom lamp, and all was well in that room, Mother came in, threw herself in her chair by the window, and lit a cigarette. At such times, in a state of passion, Mother could sit for hours, simply staring out the window, and smoking; we would not have disturbed her, but crept quietly off to bed, except we were ravenous with hunger, like street urchins, and guessed that Mother must be hungry too. So we banged about in the kitchen preparing a simple meal of eggs, cheese, bread (Mother had dismissed our housekeeper earlier that day), and brought it into Mother's bedroom, and we arrayed ourselves at her feet on the carpet, all of us eating together, very tired, yet happy; at least, relieved to be back home again. Seeing that Mother was relaxed, though still sullen and brooding, one of us dared ask, "Will we have to go to the train station, another time?" and Mother fixed us with that single all-enveloping gaze, and said, "One day, you won't have to ask."

Murder

The morning following the news of the murder the children's uncle went to work as usual at the post office and their parents wouldn't talk about what had happened except to say yes a woman was killed but it's no one we know. The children understood that the woman who'd been killed was a friend of their uncle Dennie's though that wasn't said exactly, or not said in their presence or in their precise earshot. Still, they understood something was wrong, or, if not wrong, not right: the atmosphere in the house wasn't right: and it had to do with Uncle Dennie but it had to do even more with no one acknowledging it had to do with Uncle Dennie and above all—how the children knew this, they could not have said: years later, recollecting, could not begin to say—no one mentioning or even hinting to Uncle Dennie that it had, or had *not*, to do with him. The children were well aware of their parents on the telephone a good deal more than usual, and the telephone ringing a good deal more than usual, but the calls were always made, or taken, discreetly, doors closed and perhaps even locked against the children and none of them—there were two boys and a girl, ages ranging from six to eleven—dared press an ear against the door to eavesdrop. Relatives dropped by the house, seemingly by accident, and a few friends, so the children began to hear things such as how was Dennie taking it and had the police kept him long and were they going to question him further and was there any talk of—and here the voices dropped, the words became inaudible—and the children had to guess it was *was there any talk of him being arrested.* The answer was no not yet. Or the answer was no not so far as we know. Or, *we* don't know—Dennie refuses to talk about it.

The murdered woman, white, had lived in a welfare hotel in what was predominantly a black neighborhood. It was said she'd had four children by four different men and it was a matter of public record that she'd been taken into police custody the previous year for having beaten her two-year-old son so badly he'd had to be hospitalized for six weeks. The charge, subsequently dropped, was aggravated assault, and after the woman's death neighbors told police conflicting stories—yes she'd been guilty of that crime and numerous others against her children which suggested it was only equitable she'd been beaten to death by one or another of her lovers; no she hadn't been guilty of that crime only guilty of shielding the actual criminal who was one or another of her lovers—it was really he who'd beaten the two-year-old one night in a drunken rage and the woman had taken the blame on herself for being a bad mother.

When the woman was found dead early Sunday morning in a weedy rubble-strewn lot near her apartment building no one in the neighborhood or among her acquaintance was surprised—it was going to happen sooner or later—what else can you expect—though a fair number expressed pity, and regret, and even sadness, since in some quarters at least the woman was well liked, admired for what was called her personality, her sense of humor, her guts. At the time of her death she hadn't been living full-time with any specific man but there were several—or more than several—she saw frequently and one of them was Dennis Brewer who worked at the post office and lived with his brother and his brother's family and had acquired a reputation in recent years—though not an official public record— for being "strange." The murdered woman had met Dennis Brewer in a local tavern which was the way she met most of her men friends, according to the testimony of witnesses. She might have been seen in Brewer's company the night of the murder though she might have been seen in the company of two or three other men as well—testimony varied. But no one knew, or wanted to say, which one of the men had killed her: beaten her so badly around the head she hadn't been identified for hours.

The children's uncle Dennie was home from overseas and home from the state university and it looked like home to stay but his family was the kind where personal questions usually weren't asked in order to spare embarrassment. He had gone to the university with the intention of studying art but for some unexplained reason he was back home, and working at the post office, after the first semester: it was said he hadn't even registered in an art course but it wasn't said why and Dennie's own testimony was vague and ambiguous—things hadn't worked out he'd said with a shrug and a tight twist of his mouth as if there was a joke here of some kind but you'd better not laugh. Sometimes Dennie was the shiest most considerate most courteous young man on earth and sometimes, no one could predict when, he was sullen and brooding and "kept to himself" at work, at home, in one or another of the local bars he frequented. Sometimes he drank moderately, sometimes he drank too much. Sometimes he was sweet, sometimes he was mean. He *was* extremely intelligent, overqualified for his job, which was part of his "strangeness."

The children would remember their young uncle as gentle and kindly if occasionally absentminded. When he spoke to them, however, he always spoke carefully and precisely as if words mattered; as if *they* mattered. In this way he wasn't like other adults and they seemed to sense that this meant Dennie wasn't quite right whatever "right" meant.

He was tall and heavyset, muscular in the shoulders and torso, with crimped-looking hair that seemed to lift from his forehead in an expression of vague surprise. A tight look to the mouth which accentuated its smallness and he wore black-rimmed plastic glasses that gave him a sharp focused look as if he were staring, staring really hard, and not always liking what he saw.

The children knew from exchanges overheard between Dennie and their parents that Dennie worried a good deal about people talking of him behind his back and that these worries were systematically ridiculed by their parents, particularly by their father who was, after all, Dennie's older brother—older by thirteen years—even when the worries might have had some substance in fact: people did talk about Dennie a good deal, and told stories about him, not meant to be malicious but just entertaining, Dennie this and Dennie that and who would have predicted, he'd been well liked in high school, and even a member of the varsity football team, he'd end up like this—the way he seemed to be ending up. Which is to say living in his brother's house as he did aged twenty-nine (in a spare bedroom at the rear the children's mother insisted should be thoroughly cleaned at least every two weeks and if Dennie didn't want to do it *she* would do it to do it and Dennie would be hurt or insulted or angered saying of course *he'd* clean the room *he* was perfectly capable of running a vacuum cleaner but for some reason days would go by and Dennie wouldn't get around to cleaning the room so the children's mother would get upset and the children's father would get involved and words were exchanged and finally in a burst of energy Dennie would clean the room slamming the vacuum cleaner around and talking loudly and angrily to himself and that would be that for a few weeks until the problem reasserted itself) and with no friends male or female he'd dare bring home to meet his family and no prospects for the future. He avoided his old high school friends, for instance. Actually turned away, crossed streets, to avoid saying hello. And if he was cornered in a store he could behave rudely in his haste, you might say his desperation, to get away.

In his brother's house he might have been behaving strangely all along but who could say?—the children, newly aware of their uncle, as so many observers were newly and keenly and nervously aware of him, could see it was "strange" that Uncle Dennie never read the Sunday paper, including the color comics, the way the rest of the family did. He didn't watch television with them, ever: not even weekend football or the World Series. He didn't talk much and was likely to mumble inaudible replies when the children's mother spoke to him. There were times when he kept to his room refusing supper and there were times when he overate, gorged himself at the table making no pretense of listening to the children's parents' conversation just biting and chewing and swallowing, moisture glistening in his eyes. It was said he'd gone without food when he was sick in the army hospital or was he sick from going without food? Those evenings he was at home he'd spend looking through art books from the public library—he took the same ones out again and again since the library's holdings were limited: Van Gogh, Rembrandt, Dürer, Matisse, Picasso—and doing pencil drawings in his sketchbook which he'd tear out and crumple and toss away. (Which was how the children knew about them, finding them in the trash. Uncle Dennie's drawings were quick and careless-seeming and never complete, just parts of heads, bodies, mysterious geometrical figures half human and half machine. The paper was usually badly crumpled as if he'd closed it in his fist.)

The morning after the news of the murder the children's uncle went to work as usual, and the morning after that, and nothing seemed to be changed except, in the house, there was a certain strained atmosphere, and Dennie kept to himself in his room and the children's mother cautioned them not to trouble him without explaining exactly why except to say that something—"something sad"—had happened to him. Telephone calls came for Dennis Brewer from people who wouldn't identify themselves and when the children's mother or father refused to put Dennie on the phone the callers became abusive, used obscene and threatening language. The children's mother became nervous, frightened, began to worry about something happening—and about any of them, particularly the children, being home alone with Dennie in the house. The children's father was annoyed with her saying she didn't really think Dennie'd done it did she?—and she said what about you, what do *you* think?— and the children, overhearing, understood what was being implied though they weren't altogether certain what was being said. This went on for a week, two weeks. It was true that Dennie had been questioned by police, interrogated was probably the more accurate term, it was true he was a suspect perhaps even a leading suspect though—of course—none of this was official, not in the local newspaper at least, for which, as the children's mother said repeatedly, thank God. The children learned of it to their excitement and dread though they were of course forbidden to say anything about it to their uncle to whom in any case, now, they rarely spoke, though they regarded him—when they had the opportunity—with extreme interest. At school their classmates began asking was their uncle the man who killed that woman? was their uncle going to go to jail? to the electric chair? and they said please mind your own business. But they loved it, those weeks. They'd remember those weeks for a long long time.

Dennie himself never talked about the situation. Never talked about where he went when summoned to police headquarters, or how long he was retained, or what was said to him, or what seemed to be developing. He was quieter than usual but not exceptionally quieter than usual and he never gave any indication (not even to the children's father, as it was afterward disclosed) of what he was going through whatever it was he was going through except some edginess now and then which matched the general household mood. The children's mother was particularly skittish—starting when Dennie entered a room, though she surely knew he was in the house; shrinking involuntarily from him when they passed in the hall. At the same time she made a point of being, in his presence, so warm, friendly, cheerful, solicitous, he was no longer capable of looking her in the face. He carried himself with an air of caution and irony but he was always in control. He did not, for instance, lean his elbows on the dining room table and look at them each in turn to inquire politely did they think he was a murderer—were they curious to know, *was* he the murderer?

Though one night he did ask the children's father—in a voice that was nearly inaudible—Would you like me to move out?—and the children's father said quickly, No, no of course not.

And after a pause: Where would you go, if you did?

And then the murderer was arrested. And confessed. (A local man, a resident too of the welfare hotel.) And though Dennis Brewer was innocent (presumably) people continued to view him with a certain degree of suspicion. It was as if the man had absorbed and been contaminated by evil as freshly laundered white sheets, hung out to dry, might absorb and be contaminated by polluted air. Even the children could not shake off the expectation, or was it the perverse unspoken hope, that their uncle Dennie had done something special—was something special. Though of course they knew better. As everyone knew better.

No one's fault, the children's father was to say, in time. He did not see that it was *his* fault, for instance.

In any case Dennie moved out of the house, with no warning,

only a few days after the murderer, the "real" murderer it might be said, was taken into custody. He loaded his car and a U-Haul van and moved across town to a rented room which it was speculated he shared with another person: in some versions a woman very like the slut of a woman who'd been killed, in other versions a man very like Dennie himself. He quit his job at the post office and got a job as a nightwatchman in a factory then after a few weeks quit that job and left town without saying good-bye to anyone and went to live in a city a considerable distance away—or so it was reported: Dennie himself sent no word to his brother, never troubled to call. Isn't that just like him, the children's father said repeatedly—just *like* him. Living under my roof those years and this is the thanks I get—

Two years later at Christmastime the children received a Christmas card from their uncle, postmarked Salt Lake City, Utah. What was Uncle Dennie doing in Utah?—so far away? The card was of a pot-bellied white-whiskered Santa Claus in an utterly conventional pose, a sack of presents over his shoulder, a cheap card sold off a drugstore rack, signed with just the name: *Dennie*. No message, no Christmas wishes, not even an expression of love: just *Dennie*. In a hand that didn't much resemble his but must have been his for whose would it have been otherwise?

Insomnia

A call came from my brother in the hospital: Help me to die.

You gave up expecting smiles from him—the facial muscles had atrophied. Also his eyelids couldn't close completely, he'd be watching you always. Even with the glassy eyeball rolled up blank you knew he was watching.

I said, I can't be tricked more than once! and hung up the phone. Remembering my brother had already died, and he'd done it without my help.

Alone of the family I was entrusted with discovering the secrets of the Body. Trying not to pitch forward and hit my forehead on the edge of the cadaver table, the fumes were so powerful, but here's the scalpel glittering in my hand laying open tissue and striated muscle and bright-dyed arteries and ghost-pale cords of nerves; and, in time, following the outline provided by the dissection lab instructor, liver, kidneys, intestines, a heart. In time, eyeballs and a tongue. A skull to be halved by hacksaw. A brain.

My teammates joked. They were male, they joked. Did the cadaver have a name, does a brain have a name, what is the sense in which a brain "smiles"? Could you gaze tenderly into mirrors for years and years and years knowing that one day a kid with a syringe in brash-trembling fingers is going to inflate your eyeballs and dissect the muscles around the eyes so you can't close them ever ever again?

Our cadaver's secret name (the instructor was not to know) was Grandma.

When you can't sleep the place of hell is bed.

Hearing the dark waves lapping around you and beneath you, radiant-dark plumes of sleep, delicious drowning-sleep but you float unable to sink into the waves, it's a curse like tiny electric jolts and flashes in the brain, such jolts and flashes *are* the brain, the living biochemical brain, the mystery-brain that's also the soul. But you can't sleep.

Eyes shut tight for the descent into the dark water and hands folded on your breastbone in the classic prayer position. As if that might help.

Hours and nights tick by in such paralysis for the first principle of insomnia is: To beg for sleep is always to be denied it.

Which brought me unwelcome temptations. Caused me to turn up in places I never meant and at hours of the night not my choice.

And on the bright-lit bus, and the subway, hurrying to get to my brother before he died a second time without my knowledge.

If I went to Rusty's down behind the hospital there'd be guys who laid their hands on me, one beer and my head fractured, split right along the midsagittal plane, and every giggly thought spilling out. If I went to the all-night cafeteria The Möbius it was only coffee I drank, a full day and a full night unsleeping so why not coffee, delicious tarry-black coffee, and my spiral notebooks to memorize, a hive of buzzing facts to lodge safe inside my head where they could be neither plundered nor mislaid. Except: at The Möbius there were eerie metallic Möbius-mobiles hanging from the ceiling on invisible wires, quivering, semirotating overhead, the Möbius strip is the principle of topological horror, time without end, consciousness without end, eternal unsleeping. So sitting at a table you had to endure your eyes glancing upward jumpy and nerved-up as the mobiles fluttered in mockery of all human effort.

It was 1969. I was twenty-two years old. A girl with thyroid eyes, jutting pelvis bones, straggly hair like bleached-out marsh grass. I was in terror of the long subway ride then the bus ride to my brother so I'd be pushing my tray along the gleaming rail at The Möbius, 3:30 A.M. of a weekday, a Styrofoam cup filled to the brim with bitter black coffee on my tray and I'd feel with a shiver the eyes come up, trout eyes, silvery pike eyes, lifting. Readying to strike.

No one's fault, the lusts you arouse in others.

We'd observed human beings that were suction mouths and catheters emptying into plastic bags, the guys observed testicles wizened to the size of peas and pebble hard or swollen and ulcerated like poisoned Hallowe'en apples so naturally they had thoughts of their own testicles and their own immortality, oh Jesus God. And there I'd come out stumbling without my glasses. Eyes blinking and swimmy with nearsightedness and my skin chalky white and the shadowy sockets of my eyes urging them to think of blackened eyes, pummeled breasts, belly, balled-up fists and penises stiff as rods and mean-hooked.

One night I'd gotten as far as the subway stairs before turning back, I ran seven blocks to The Möbius and sweating inside my sheepskin jacket I was stumbling, trying to pull out a spindly-legged chair, little tongue-flames of dreams were darting at me because I hadn't slept for a day and a night and my mouth was dry as death and a guy I didn't know except for the brotherly insomnia-eyes was hanging over me, close so that I could smell his stale breath, uninvited he sat down across from me at the table so small our knees knocked, he was grinning, he was shy behind big-knuckled hands raised to hide his teeth, "That funny scar on your forehead, how'd you get it?" he asked, and I touched the scar without knowing what I did, pale sickle of a scar like spittle above my left eye which usually I was careful to keep hidden under bangs but the wind had blown my hair to hell so he'd seen, possibly other nights he'd been observing too, seemed to know, I wondered *was* this in fact my brother returned to me in the shape of a lanky slope-shouldered man of maybe thirty with a bony forehead, hollowed-out nostrils, bad teeth, yes but his eyes were silky brunette eyes and beautiful, that glisten of doom impossible to resist, so I fingered the scar as if to hide it, where once to both punish myself and calm my nerves when I was fifteen years old I'd slashed at my skin with a razor—one of those therapeutic acts that consume themselves in the execution and need never be repeated nor even explained for who would understand who required an explanation and who, understanding, would require an explanation? At the time of the scarring I'd told my family and whoever inquired that I had fallen off my bicycle and cut my forehead on a curb but now I said shyly, "It was just something I needed to do once, for a reason, it isn't important now."

He called himself Radar Ray. That luminous-fish sort of skin.

He said, grinning behind his knuckles, "Yeah, honey. I thought it was something cool like that."

About nerves. You have *nerve*, meaning you're brave. Or you're *nervy*, meaning you're pushy. Or you're *nerved-up* meaning you're excitable and readying for something to happen. Yes but there are *nerves*, *nerve cells* cable-stitched into *nerves*, true physical things, *nerves* whose names you can memorize strung out like Christmas lights inside the flesh so we were burrowing into Grandma's fatty thigh and she never felt a thing, you steel yourself thinking they'll flinch and scream and bleed but no, this is death, this isn't even death this is deadness, dead meat, and so inside the thigh there was this strange sinewy thing, like cord, but like a miniature tube too, tough and ghost pale and one of us asked the instructor what it was and he told us and we laughed saying, "Oh—a nerve is *real*," it became a joke among us because while you know a nerve is real you somehow don't believe it until you lay it bare with your own scalpel and severe it neat as cutting a thread.

The things you know and the things you can comprehend.

The things you know not to say aloud but hear yourself saying.

Like confessing to Radar Ray my old secret, not having meant even to speak to him, acknowledge him—I'd known he was a junky dropout from medical school, he supplied everyone I knew with amphetamines and downers—and there I was looking him full in the face, my eyes smoky—dilated from no sleep and my mouth like a bruise, and this he took for a sign, and was justified.

Later, he was to show me the pale serrated scars on the inside of his left wrist. Poking his narrow wrist out of his sleeve as if cautious of rejection the way a guy unzips his pants unless he's drunk and angry and without fear, there's the moment when your eyes pinch in revulsion or turn soft, damp-dilated eyes their sisters would never give them, so Radar Ray showed me his scars in the most graceful gesture I'd ever seen in a man, I had no choice but to whisper, "Oh yes."

Why he called himself that name, silly self-mocking name, his lips curling pronouncing that name, I don't know. I never asked.

He'd meant to be a brain surgeon but he feared the brain. Couldn't touch the brain. Almost puked examining brain in slides, had to crouch with his head between his knees when it was hacksaw day in the lab, sawing skulls in half. He was a burnt-out case he said; "burnt-out" was an expression he favored; it had a certain reverence on his tongue; it had the tone of a mother's tender forgiveness. He told me, "There are things we do that have to be done, there's reasons for doing them, but it's years later and you forget."

My brother was becoming increasingly impatient with the telephone, sometimes he'd speak directly in my ear, my head on my sweaty pillow and whichever ear was exposed was vulnerable to him. He was dying, but he wasn't dying fast enough. As the striped muscles degenerate and are replaced by fibrous tissue or fat the dying can take a long time. Respiratory failure or infection or heart failure but it can take a long time but I told him that's an old story: you hear it all the time. I told him I couldn't help him, I wasn't the one to help him. I refused to steal a syringe like a junky nor would I purchase one, on principle.

My brother said, But I'd do it for you.

My brother said, Please.

There were nights I didn't bother to undress. Lay down on my bed in shirt, sweater, slacks. Reasoning that if I wasn't undressed I would save myself time dressing when I got up and probably I'd be getting up fairly soon, or, if I wasn't undressed and so seemingly not expecting sleep sleep might catch me unaware.

Sometimes it seemed to work. Not a deep healthful sleep but thin slivers of sleep, flashes of dreams like playing cards dealt by a rapid hand and then I'd be jolted awake by a noise out in the street or a murmur in my ear, Please please oh please, I lay perfectly still hoping I might be drawn down into sleep again, there's a way in which sleep is like God's grace, it happens to you, it can't be willed or begged or even prayed for, God bestows such blessings where He will.

Not that I believed in God because I didn't. My brother in his death bed where his breathing was being done for him and when the priest gave him communion he had to help him with the wafer on his tongue making sure his tongue got back inside his mouth where the saliva would melt the Host.

You don't believe. But you do these things anyway because there aren't any other things to do in their place.

So I'd lie there hoping for sleep and even if it wasn't a true sleep, just teasing flashes of dreams, I reasoned that that was infinitely better than no sleep at all; the extinction of consciousness for a single second is infinitely better than no extinction at all; cutting the Möbius strip in two with a scissors—so it's cut! I told myself that I could endure in this way for years attending lectures and doing the lab work and studying for exams and taking exams and continuing to score near the top of the class so they'd forgive me for not dying like my brother, or in his place, and he'd forgive me if he knew. That wild relief at not being him. That secret happiness, that shame.

Didn't change my clothes for days, didn't bathe. Even left my shoes on, some nights, lace-up waterproofed shoes like a hiker's ideal for tramping through the slush. The kind of thick-soled shoes you can trust to take you where you don't even know you want to go.

"If you don't sleep," said Radar Ray, "you're gonna burn out."

Beautiful mad eyes locked into mine and his thumbs on me, oh

Jesus oh don't ever stop. And then I did sleep, the two of us sleeping
on my bed, sleep heavy as death my mouth drooping open the way
a corpse's will do if it isn't wired shut and my skin clammy cool, the
heartbeat very slow, retreating. Oh Jesus oh thank you God oh
don't ever stop, let me sleep forever.

But then, other nights, Radar Ray wasn't my friend, suspicious of
me, searching through the rooms looking for "bugs."

He said, "Look, you: don't ever mock me."

I said, "Why would I mock you? I'm not the kind."

Framing my face in his strong lean fingers, saying, "All cunts are
'the kind.' " But he was smiling.

I began to be frightened of him. But he'd come around, I'd open
the door, back he'd come insinuating himself into me like one of
those dreams razor quick as playing cards. Sometimes he was melancholy and gentle, sometimes he was rough, talking talking talking
nonstop with manic acuity insisting we'd known each other back
in grade school hadn't we and I said I didn't think so, we aren't the
same age are we? hadn't gone to the same school had we? but Radar
Ray didn't seem to hear insisting he'd known me and I'd known
him, we were fated, we'd been brother-sister lovers in another
lifetime too he was convinced, certain dreams he'd had suggested it,
he believed it had been Egypt: ancient Egypt: his eyes not so beautiful now with their mad damp glisten but I could not look away.

Insomnia: the glaring face of God you don't want to look at, you'll
be struck blind.

Insomnia: where you go with certain indissolvable truths.

I stole a syringe after all, I loaded it with phenol, the preservative
with which the cadavers were coated that was also a powerful
anesthetic—if you got it on your fingers in dissection lab your
fingers would go numb. My reasoning was: I would not be poisoning
my brother, merely injecting his veins with a relaxant that would
cease the operations of his lungs and heart. He was so fucking
weary, he'd told me, of his lungs and heart.

If you can't bring yourself to do it out of love, said my brother,
voice heavy with sarcasm as in the old days, do it out of duty.

Yes, I said.

I have a gross anatomy exam tomorrow morning but yes.

It was the heaviest text, *Principles of Gross Anatomy*, there I sat hunched over it on my knees riding the subway squinting reading and rereading the same teasing paragraph I'd already marked weeks ago in code, differing shades of ink for differing degrees of emphasis, I was desperate to memorize all I could but the meanings of sentences, even of individual words began to elude me, the subway car's lights flickered and there was a faint smell of old vomit and I began to sweat and my feet in the hiker's shoes began to trace tight little circles on the floor, clockwise then counterclockwise, little Möbius strips of motion, to keep the beating of my heart in check.

Repeatedly I slipped my hand inside my sheepskin jacket where the precious syringe was wrapped in yards of gauze. I saw how the other passengers in the car, most of them male, regarded me suspiciously but they hadn't the ability to see through fabric thick as sheepskin and suede.

My brother in his hospital bed was beginning to be impatient. I didn't want to look at him too closely for fear of what I might see.

The stations clattered by, the subway cars were nearly empty now. It was after one o'clock in the morning of a weekday.

Toward two o'clock I hurried to change to another line, a line that would carry me out of the city and into another district, the subway train plunged through a tunnel beneath a river and I could feel the pressure of the water hammering against my ears. The other line appeared older: the car I blundered into was defaced with graffiti in Day-Glo colors and a drunken bewhiskered man lay happily sprawled across several seats. I did not want to look at the other passengers—there were only five or six of them, all male. Here the stench was of fresh vomit to reprimand me for my squeamishness in the other car.

As a medical student bound to excel I had already learned the first principle of caring for others: in all matters physical you must lay aside your squeamishness along with your humanity.

Huddling close to one of the exit doors I opened *Principles of Gross Anatomy* on my lap turning to the same page, the same paragraph, the same sentences like fishhooks in my vision. My brother's voice hummed with the noise of the subway, words now and then distinct, You know I can't die without you he was saying, or just Help help oh please, and I clenched my jaws so I wouldn't speak out loud, never in my worst insomniac periods did I speak out loud to myself in public places and I tried to keep my facial expression neutral since tics, twitches, and grimaces are a clear signal that total loss of control is imminent.

Radar Ray had mused in his most lucid voice that certain truths of science meant to free us from superstition and bondage to the past are just too hard finally to bear, but he'd laughed immediately showing yellow wolf teeth. There was often laughter between us.

The train moved so slowly I worried I would never get to the station where in any case I'd have to catch a suburban bus and ride several miles into the night, the machinery of the train several times seemed to be breaking down and once there was a delay of twenty excruciating minutes and everyone in the car sat rigid in worried silence except the rowdy drunk who muttered to himself recounting old arguments he'd won guffawing in triumph. Up on the surface of the Earth it was still winter: it had been winter when my brother was first diagnosed with his illness years ago: it had been winter for a very long time. Weeks of sleeplessness had left a residue of ashes in my mouth. Hairs like wires grew ticklish in my armpits, on my legs, at my crotch. I had hoped to take a bath that night; I'd hoped to shave the hairs from my body; to wash away the grime and the smell of my body; to wash my matted hair, brush and comb it lovingly as I'd done when I inhabited a body; but there had not been time.

Now we were on the island moving aboveground the train moved slowly as if impeded by air resistance. In the greasy window beside me my own reflection glowered, bulky sheepskin jacket, windblown hair but no face.

When your body wastes away it's analogous to the tide going out: what's left behind is debris.

In this lurching antiquated car the momentum of Earth was distractingly perceptible. It's known that Earth moves swiftly through space turning on its axis thus if you are traveling above it at a sufficient speed as it falls away and you fall toward it drawn by gravity you will never strike its surface, you'll float above it even as you are falling toward it, "floating" and "falling" being easily confused and this phenomenon I began to feel distinctly, the ancient curse of gravity on human flesh. I spoke bitterly to my brother, It's gravity that's to blame not me, it's gravity that is Time too, keeping you alive when you want to die and killing you when you'd wanted to live.

He turned empty mollusk eyes toward me, blind inside the drooping lids. Oh God I saw he was just a head now, or nearly: why hadn't anyone told me: a skull with tight-stretched skin covering it, a boy's features wizened to those of an elderly creature, and the torso not much larger than the head, shoulders just bones like a wire coat hanger under the flesh and the neck like a plucked chicken's, that skinny. He must have had a stomach, an abdomen, bowels but I could not see much there. His arms and legs were just sticks— maybe eight inches long—why hadn't anyone told me, but don't be sentimental since there are certain truths of science and human experience meant to free us from bondage, why not stare steadily, why not say Yes I see: yes I will: and I opened my mouth to speak to my brother but the respirator to which he was attached hissed and rattled like the train, and its lights flickered too, went out for a few seconds then glared up again, and the drunken man roused himself to sing happily, as if it were daylight, dawn—

Five-and-plenty blackpigs!
backed in a sty!

—until one of the other passengers, a kid with a shaved head, screamed him into silence.

The train plunged into a tunnel. My growing desperation was my need for a restroom: my kidneys ached: why be sentimental: the mollusk eyes could not see me anyway.

In The Möbius, that first night, this guy I didn't know brushed his fingertips against the scar on my forehead reading it like Braille, icy touch and I laughed pushing his hand away but later he asked was it time for us to leave and I said all right though that wasn't what I meant to say, I'd meant to say No. And though I did not intend to accompany this person anywhere that was what I did, or found myself doing. Radar Ray: but don't mock: he can mock himself but it's dangerous for anyone else to mock him, right?—you know that's right. Quickly and quietly he spoke but I heard the manic heat rippling beneath. He said, I've been watching you for a while and you've been watching me, and I laughed with my mouth as if this were just the usual jokey banter, he was leading me along an alley, across a back street and into another alley narrow as a footpath then we were standing belly to belly in our bulky jackets, there came his hard thumbs and sly skull smile and he kissed my lips light as a moth, he closed his long lean fingers around my throat and I stood perfectly still, I seemed to know that was the wisest course. His breath was ashes but something sweet like decay, it was a breath I could endure, so like my own. Another time he kissed me saying, Why don't you kiss back, honey—I can feel you thinking too hard, and his fingers tightened slightly, only slightly, knowing human anatomy Radar Ray's big thumb naturally knew the carotid artery which teasing he caressed: but only teasing.

Then I kissed him hungrily back, I opened my mouth, all my insides to him. Knowing then why I loved my insomnia: because it was mine: because it made me see that other people are no more real than the beautiful dreams they supplant.

Love, Forever

He was crazy about her he insisted and he certainly behaved that way when they were together, and alone. Did he! But he wasn't crazy about her three kids. Don't get me wrong he said it isn't anything personal, your kids are sweet kids, real nice, and Sherri's gonna be a real knockout, but I'm just not the type, y'know?—my wifc and I split over that, she wanted kids and I didn't, she found a guy who did and that's okay with me, y'know?—that's just how it is with some guys.

She was gazing hurt and eyes brimming with tears deep into his eyes. But said, softly, I know.

And she didn't hold it against him, how could she. Telling her straight out how it was with him, no lies or subterfuge. Not like some guys. (Not like her ex-husband.) Just laying his cards down, calm and clear and no excuses, so you could see what's what and were spared making an asshole of yourself. So, she appreciated that. She cried a little, but she appreciated that. Framing his face in her hands like an actress gazing into those blue eyes like sapphires whispering another time, I know, and solemnly she'd kissed his lips and he'd remember it, that kiss: that kiss he could not guess was a pledge.

Oh, I know!—but I love you anyway forever.

The entire day, the sun was hidden behind clouds, one of those gauzy gray days you feel like screaming but she was calm, she was

in control. Six-year-old Tommy ran inside when the school bus let
him off all excited saying the bus driver had almost hit a buck in the
fog and she smiled and kissed him and walked past as if she hadn't
heard. She's been smiling all day. It wasn't practice, it was her
natural self: as, in high school, she'd smiled all the time. She was
waiting for a phone call, she'd left a message on the answering
service of one of the girls she used to work with, when she was
working, and when the call came she had something planned to say
she'd memorized, a strange man prowling the woods behind the
trailer, a man with a beard, or maybe without a beard, probably a
hunter, she hadn't wanted to stare out at him and wasn't worried
really but she'd mention it, then talk of something else. Not too
much detail—that gave you away. From TV you learned that.

She called *him*, too: knowing he wouldn't be home.

Just to hear his voice on the answering tape. Just his voice,
sometimes—that was enough.

And hanging up, quietly. No message.

She had the gun ready. She didn't believe in firearms but it was
a .22 Ruger pistol a guy had given her for protection, when she'd
moved out here alone with the kids. She knew the precise spot in
the river to toss it where nobody would find it in a million million
years. She put on gloves, old rubber dishwashing gloves she'd be
throwing away, too. She was wearing a warm sweatshirt, long
sleeves. It was eleven P.M. and the kids were sleeping, a dark night
with no moon and everything quiet back in the woods. She hadn't
even had the TV on. Tommy, who was so excitable, naturally had
to be first. She went into his room where he was sleeping open-
mouthed in bed, she crouched over him holding the pistol calmly,
she whispered, Sweetie? as she'd planned to wake him so he'd be
looking up, maybe sitting up, and when he opened his eyes she
pulled the trigger. Jesus, what a noise!—she hadn't counted on so
much noise. Her ears ringing.

Tommy died at once, she believed. A bullet point-blank through
his chest, thus no suffering. She'd planned that.

Next was Sherri, four years old. Pale blond hair like her
mommy's, and her mommy's button nose. Sherri slept in Mommy's
bedroom where the baby was also, in his crib, and the gunshot noise

had been so loud Sherri was naturally awake, out of bed, screaming,
Mommy? Mommy?—and she ran inside, trying to stay calm, swallowing, but her voice rising shrill, It's okay, honey! Mommy's here,
it's okay! And she fired at the little girl, it wasn't exactly clear what
happened but there was one bullet in the chest yet more screaming,
and a second bullet in the chest and still more screaming, and now
she was maybe losing it just a little, panting, stooping over the
fallen writhing child to press the barrel against the top of the child's
head and to squeeze the trigger again.

And the baby. Baby Seth. Seven months old. In his crib, in the
corner of the room—that wasn't going to be hard! Baby Seth had
wakened of course in all the commotion but hadn't begun yet to
cry. It was that kind of baby—a little slow.

At the rear entrance to the hospital she ran inside screaming for
help. Somebody shot my kids! A man, a man shot my kids! And
they came out at once, no wasting time, five, six, maybe seven of
them, and saw Tommy sprawled in the front seat of the Olds, and
pulled him out to carry inside to try to save his life, and the baby,
the baby was in the front seat, too, My God there's a baby—one
of the orderlies, a big black guy, yelled, like he couldn't believe it,
and she stood there watching, this little smile on her face,
bemused—how they were all running around, not smooth and
coordinated the way you'd expect, taking the kids inside to save
their lives when, couldn't they tell?—these kids were dead.

Actually, in fact, Tommy was not dead, but dying: he'd die,
officially, that's to say when they couldn't resuscitate him, and his
heart had stopped forever, at four A.M. of the next day.

The baby *was* dead.

It had been a listless baby, conceived not in love but spite.

So much commotion at the rear of the emergency unit of the
hospital, everybody gaping, like lights had come on brighter like on
TV, and maybe in fact they had, and she was standing there by the
automatic doors, watching, in her blood-soaked clothes, her new
jeans fitting her tight as if she'd been poured into them, and her Led
Zeppelin sweatshirt, and the spike-heeled cowhide glamour boots—
she was blinking, smiling just faintly, as if all she was doing *was*

watching, calm, and curious to see how it would go, as the medical crew would testify at her trial. Where she should have been—what? Screaming, sobbing like a madwoman, running back and forth, trying to touch her kids?—was that what another mother would do, in this situation? Or was she, you could argue this, in shock?

But, no, she was reported to have called out, following them into the hospital, Nothing but the best for these kids! And she'd sounded scolding, but sly. Her eyes making the rounds of the waiting room where everybody's eyes were sure on *her.*

But then, my God, it came to her like a blow: little Sherri was still in the car! Out there, in the car!

Nobody'd seen Sherri. She must have slipped off the backseat during the wild skidding ride nine miles to town, lying on the floor hidden from view and the goddamn careless medical crew hadn't even noticed. So, she was excited now, she had to yell to get their attention, grabbing one of the nurses by the arm, digging her nails in hard, Hey, my little girl!—don't forget *her.*

The look on their faces. Almost, you'd have to laugh.

It *was* weird, though, and she'd never understand it—forgetting Sherri like that. Sherri was the one Mommy had always loved best.

Old Dog

There he lies, in the grass, in his habitual place, waiting for you.

It has been years. He is aged, near blind. But he waits. In the grass, in his usual place. For you.

He is part collie and part German shepherd. His fur has coarsened and feels like wires, dry and ungiving, to the touch. Its luster has long since faded; it's that drab dun color of a deer's winter coat. He is lying, forelegs extended, shoulders and head quivering erect. His eyes are rheumy, as if covered with a thin film of mucus. His muzzle is gray, his lower lip unnaturally swollen. From time to time his nose twitches and his ears prick up alertly at imaginary sounds; actual sounds, unless loud and immediate, he is less likely to hear.

He has become an old dog, you would hardly recognize him now. The bony haunches, the lusterless eyes, ribs showing through his fur. When he'd been a puppy, his small eager body was charged as if with electricity; he seemed never to sleep, nor even to rest. His eyes shone with a doggy intelligence and good-will. His feelings were easily hurt but his hurts easily forgotten. He loved you above all things, and has never outgrown that love. You were his fate, you alone. Though this was not a fact you would have acknowledged.

In some creatures, love is a clock we set ticking. We see it start but are rarely around to see it end.

You have been gone for years. You are not likely to return. The old dog doesn't know. Or, knowing, is not one to act upon such knowledge. For what remains to him, except you? The memory of you? Your touch, your embrace, your hand rough with affection on his head, your happy, careless shouts, the smells that are you, and you only?

So, there, in his habitual place, he lies waiting. In the grass. In the cemetery. At the base of that nicely trimmed grave, in the shadow of that tasteful granite marker. Flies, bees, gnats annoy him, or annoy his skin, which twitches to repulse them, even as his eyes take no notice. He sleeps, and he wakes, and he sleeps, waiting for you, a perpetual waiting, and perhaps there is no longer much difference between his sleep and his waking. From time to time his nose lifts in expectation and his ears prick up at an imaginary sound—his own, old name, perhaps, in your voice.

The Artist

I began modestly with still lifes, here in my studio. The logic of the *still life* is self-evident: its beauty is likely to be the classical beauty of form; it does not move or reveal new and unanticipated facets of being; its will is at all times subservient to the artist's own; its decay is slow enough as to seem imperceptible. That first summer, my eighteenth, in an ecstasy of concentration I painted eggplants— dozens, hundreds! Gorgeous gleaming purple-iridescent eggplants filled canvas after canvas, taking on, by the strokes of my brush, the mysterious contours and inner radiance of noble forms of being! (As if, as a critic for an influential Roman newspaper later claimed, Caravaggio himself had been reborn, turning his genius to still lives.) In a delirium of boyish energy, with no purpose beyond the transposition of *life* into *art*, the *perishable* into the *imperishable*, I also painted pumpkins, tomatoes, peppers, broccoli, cauliflowers. . . . In the garden behind our family villa, the vines began to shrivel; the plants, some of them quite gigantic, grew wizened; one might have thought it a natural consequence of the season's change, except that the very soil, for centuries so rich, a luscious russet red, grew gray and anemic, and crumbly, dissolving to dust between one's fingers. Not even our heavy autumn rains could restore it, and one morning my sister Lucia ran into my studio, crying, "Look, Antonio! It's gone!"

To the family's astonishment, the entire hillside garden of several acres had vanished. Had erosion been eating away at it, from beneath, without our knowledge? In place of the lush, fertile garden were ugly fissures in the earth, as deep as twelve feet, the soil arid and colorless as a lunar landscape, and as lifeless. In time, spiky, bristly weeds grew there—if you look out this casement window you can see them, so stiff and unyielding, even the north winds can't sway them.

My elegant paintings, however, sold—sold wonderfully. Especially in Rome, where foreign travelers visit, wealthy Americans in particular.

Next, I turned my scrupulous attention upon the family parrot, Sheba: an exotic creature imported from Brazil, with exquisite green, yellow, golden, and blood red feathers, and a saucy crest, and shrewd, watchful, malicious eyes. As I painted, I whistled—and Sheba playfully mimicked my whistle. Sometimes I sang, to placate her, "Pretty bird! O beautiful Sheba!" and the creature mimicked my voice, though not my words, crying, "Fool 'Tonio! Fool-fool 'Tonio!" I laughed, and Sheba echoed my laughter, though in a mocking soprano.

Why is it that household pets, especially parrots and cats, become tyrants sometimes?—willful as Indian maharajas in their domestic settings? Our beloved Sheba, thirty years old, was certainly the dominant will in our family, since Momma's death the previous year. Even Poppa, mayor of our provincial town and, by ancestral tradition, a descendent of royalty, was no match for Sheba when she exerted her will squawk-squawk-squawking to get her way.

Of course, the South American parrot is one of the wonders of the natural world. In such brilliant, dazzling, painterly beauty, any number of flaws of character are forgiven; and so it was in our household, with Sheba, whom we prized—I, Antonio, in particular.

My paintings of Sheba, sixteen of them painted within the space of a delirious two-week period, are valued as examples of "primitive genius"—"unschooled classicism"—"provincial magic." Poppa and I exhibited them at a regional fair, and all the canvases were sold; two were awarded prizes; all were written up glowingly in newspapers, and I, Antonio, to my surprise, was the subject of a profile in a national magazine. Poppa acted as my broker, negotiating with buyers of my work and putting my money in a special account in our local bank, under his name. He then gave me a fixed allowance, out of which I could buy my art supplies. "I hope you are pleased, Antonio?" Poppa asked, stroking his beard—that rich, black, bristling beard that, from earliest boyhood, I could not help but envy. "Yes, Poppa," I said quietly. "Your allowance is a very generous one, for a young man of your age and position," Poppa said, as if testing me. But I said, quietly, as before, "Yes, Poppa. Very generous."

After the heady success of the fair, I never painted another canvas with Sheba's likeness. Following the temperamental vagaries of her species, Sheba began to pick at her breast, until most of he splendid feathers there were gone; she managed to pick even at her wings and back and was soon an ugly, blood-stippled sight. Lucia, who, after Momma's death, had spoiled Sheba with all sorts of treats and special attentions, was upset at first; and then despondent. And, unaccountably, angry at *me*—"If you had not painted her so beautifully, she might still be unblemished," Lucia said. "You!— stealing her of her beauty, in the name of art!"

It was a mercy when, one day, we discovered Sheba lifeless and stiff on the floor of her cage, amid droppings and dried patches of blood. Poor thing! We all wept, including the servants.

And yet, how blissful the morning silence, uninterrupted by Sheba's cries.

I had mentioned that Poppa was mayor of our town. In fact, Poppa had been first elected to this illustrious post twenty-three years ago, but his term of office had been turbulent and marred by charges of graft and corruption; he had not sought reelection. In subsequent years, other holders of the office were similarly charged by their political rivals and enemies (for ours is a contentious province), and the most recent, preceding Poppa's second election, was sent to prison for extorting bribes and embezzlement—so that, as even Poppa's critics were forced to admit, Poppa did not appear half so bad, by comparison!

So it has always been, for centuries, seemingly for millennia, in this remote, hilly, verdant province north of Rome. Graft, corruption, mendacity, vanity! A history of infamy! Which is why the more sensitive of its progeny have traditionally turned to the Church (that is, to its ascetic orders, cloistered convents and monasteries), and to the abiding solace of art. *For what does it profit a man, that he gain the world, but lose his soul?*

Poppa, in his position as mayor, commissioned a portrait of himself, to be hung in the foyer of the mayoral residence—and who was the portraitist to be but I, Antonio! There were murmurings of nepotism and complaints that the commission was far too generous (though, by current standards, as such things are measured, the commission was not excessively high for an experienced artist, at least); but Poppa paid not the slightest heed and counseled me to behave likewise.

So, with some trepidation, I painted my own father's portrait—the first human subject I ever undertook. Dear Poppa!—a vain, blustering, overbearing man, yet touchingly direct in his egotism. "Shall I paint you as you are, Poppa," I asked politely, "or as you wish to be remembered?" Poppa, seated in the mayor's chair by an open window, his heavy head held unnaturally high and his bearing self-consciously regal, replied with childlike ingenuousness, "Why, paint me exactly as I am, silly boy—for that is how people will want to remember me."

The sittings were a strain more for me than for Poppa, who readily passed into an open-eyed daze, sated by wine and food (our sessions were midafternoon, following Poppa's enormous midday meal, which was nearly as lavish as his evening meal); or, by degrees, sank into a blissful, snoring, leaden sleep. Never had I known that painting—the wielding of a mere brush!—could be so arduous. It was as if, in painting my father, from whose veins my own rich blood had partly sprung, I was expunging, from myself, a secret part of myself, unfathomed until that time. How ugly Poppa was, for a man commonly spoken of as "handsome"—how venal, how petty, how self-important, how cruel and mendacious his features! My brush moved gropingly at first, and I ruined one canvas after another, and had to start over, in disgust, having not the patience (or, perhaps, the stomach) to rework the original image, layering it in oils until it was covered by another. Gradually, however, I came to terms with Poppa's image—with Poppa. The man's strong-boned face—his black bristling beard—his deep-socketed, dark, glaring eyes—that smiling grimace that gave his face the look of a nocturnal creature surprised and displeased by daylight: all this I managed to transfer to the canvas, painting for hours without rest, in a trance, day following day. At the conclusion of a session, Poppa merely glanced at the canvas as it began to take shape, and grunted, whether in approval or disapproval I could not know; in any case, uneducated as the man was, he had no true eye for art and did not even know, as the truism has it, what he believed he should like. He did complain of my slowness, however—"Boy, d'you think you, and I, are going to live forever?" Once seated in his cushioned chair, confident he would not be rudely interrupted (for the mayor's assistants, without exception older females, did the daily work of the office, and did it uncomplainingly, for shockingly modest salaries), Poppa quickly slipped into a daze or a doze; while I, Antonio, labored to bring forth a portrait worthy of my name.

Which, I believe, I *have* done.

Of course, I have not the original—I have only this photograph, a poor reproduction that does not begin to suggest the portrait's somber yet savage demeanor; its formal elegance; its rich chiaroscuro, "an ingenuous rendering of a petty tyrant," as one reviewer has said, "worthy of the genius of Goya."

The portrait was angrily denounced by Poppa's successor in office, thus never hung in the foyer, as intended; but it was eagerly purchased—at several times the price of the commission—by one of my New York collectors. Poor Poppa!—*he* did not arrange for the purchase, which would have pleased him enormously.

For Poppa is departed; whither he has gone, no one, not even his closest political associates, nor even the beautiful peasant woman with whom he sometimes slept, seems to know.

At our final session, Poppa slumped in his chair as usual; and I, as usual, though perhaps more intensely than usual, labored at the ugly, intransigent image on the canvas, until my arm grew so heavy I could scarcely move my brush, and my body was slick with perspiration inside my clothes. I thought of the teachings of the great Englishman Locke, who looked upon man as an object in nature, not fundamentally distinct from other objects in nature,

and wished, indeed *willed*, that the subject of my portrait, though
nominally my father, but in essence a mere composite of molecules,
atoms, and force fields of incalculable subtlety, be transposed onto
my canvas: rendered into *my* art, once and for all.

You are surprised I did not pray to God? But, like any artist of
genius, I do not believe in God. I do not believe in God because I
have no need of God—the artist's credo is that simple.

During that grueling session, however, Poppa played one of his
pranks on me. He must have woken out of his sodden sleep, seen
me fierce in concentration at the easel, and slipped away without
my noticing; oddly, for he was a large, bulky man, and hardly
graceful on his feet. But when, at last, near dusk, I looked up in
triumph, knowing my portrait was finished, I saw that Poppa was
gone—vanished! His thronelike chair was empty, though the faded
cushion bore the imprint of his solid buttocks and the head- and
armrests gleamed faintly with oil. The door to the stairs stood partly
ajar. So obsessed had I been with the painting, I had not even heard
Poppa's heavy footsteps on the stairs. I had not even had the opportunity to murmur, "Good-bye, dear Poppa!" as certainly I would
have done, had I known he was departing.

For, by a coincidence, surely, it was that very night that Poppa
disappeared from our town.

Some charged that the mayor had absconded with funds from a
mutual cache he and his political cronies had established out of
"lost"—or embezzled—municipal funds; others claimed that he
must have been abducted and later murdered—for Poppa never
reappeared, no news ever came of him, and his body, the proud
bearer of a six-hundred-year-old name, was never found.

Lucia said, simply, gazing at Poppa's portrait, "He is dead. Of
course."

Poor Poppa! But, more than that, poor Lucia! In our household, it
was she who grieved the most bitterly; yet as much out of spite, I
think, as genuine sorrow at our loss, for, being a woman, and
unmarried, she eventually inherited only a modest portion of
Poppa's estate, and her brothers the remainder. I, Antonio, the
youngest, received the most, for Poppa, even in his duplicity, had

been honest enough to allocate my own earnings as a painter to me.
(And these earnings were higher than I'd known! What a rascal,
poor Poppa.) As the months passed, Lucia not only mourned our
father, but cast veiled, reproachful eyes upon me, as if—though,
mean-spirited, purse-lipped, she never said so—my portrait of him
was in some way responsible for his death.

But in what way?—by all the paradigms of common sense?

Thus, in stealth, to record for posterity the lineaments of the
low-minded, suspicious, *paranoid* personality, so paradoxically
housed in an ample, attractive, female body, I painted Lucia's portrait, too, without her knowledge—but that is another story.

You may see her here—her likeness, that is—in this photograph:
which does not begin to do justice to the original, I'm afraid.

The original?—in a private collection, in New York City.

Now, will *you* be seated, over there? Shall we begin?

The Wig

It was in a curious motorized vehicle—resembling a small open-cockpit airplane, or a canoe with wheels—that they drove themselves to Building E in which their friend H. was convalescing.

The hospital grounds were enormous!—far larger inside than one would have judged from the outside. Shading their eyes against the sun they could scarcely make out the fifteen-foot spiked iron fence that surrounded the property.

In the entry to Building E a young black attendant seated at a desk asked to see their passes. His white uniform was stained at the cuffs. He was lean and wiry, with round schoolboy spectacles. For a nervous moment it looked as if he would not allow them into the building though their passes were initialed and seemingly in good order. Then he waved them on down the corridor and returned to his immense paperback medical textbook.

They walked quickly along the lengthy deserted corridor, speaking in whispers. Where was E-18? The numbers on the doors were faint and blurred. They passed a room through whose open doorway they saw an oldish man with gray hair seated at a small table, typing; they passed a room in which a woman of youthful middle age was seated making up her face by way of a hand mirror; another room in which a dark-haired young person—male or female, it was difficult to tell—glanced up hopefully at their approach. They decided that E-18 must have been the room belonging to the man at

148

the typewriter though that man had not appeared to resemble their friend.

And so it was!

H. had changed so drastically, they might not have recognized him. He had aged, he looked bloated, his face had turned gray and puffy like something decomposing in water. Yet his eyes were brightly alert and his hair though entirely gray now was bushy, springy, almost defiantly full—the hair of a man in the prime of life and in perfect health.

Hello hello hel*lo!*

H. was overjoyed to see them: greeting them warmly, hugging them each in turn, in his old effusive emotional way.

If he noted their expressions of shock he was gentlemanly enough to give no sign.

To their feeble questions of how are you he said, rubbing his hands briskly together, Fine! As you can see!

H. was deeply immersed, he said, in work. Revising a story. A new story? they asked eagerly. No, not new, H. said, in fact not new at all, one of the much anthologized stories he'd written in a burst of manic energy at the age of twenty-four and ever afterward regretted not having polished. He was adding several new passages, new lines of dialogue. Please read us what you've written, they begged, but at once H. became slyly evasive. He picked up from the clutter of things on his table a sample dust jacket for his next book—sassy lemon yellow with bold black print—and asked did they like it? Yes, they said enthusiastically, they liked it very much, but H. persisted, *Do* you? *Do* you? holding the jacket at arm's length as if to get it into better focus—in the window's light, the glossy yellow surface appeared to catch fire—and they repeated, Yes, though faltering a bit like men caught in lies. H. tossed the jacket down without comment but spoke for several boastful minutes of his publisher's plan for the book: H. was to travel extensively around the country promoting it which he'd never done before but was now really looking forward to. For, after all, things were different now.

They did not ask H. in what way things were different now.

H. changed the subject abruptly. With a sudden wink that

screwed up half his face like crumpled paper he said, I know why you boys are here!

They laughed uncertainly but did not ask H. why he thought they were there.

H.'s room was large and sparely furnished: a standard-issue hospital bed, sheets rumpled and pillows awry; grimy white walls and sticky, well-worn linoleum floor; nondescript vinyl-covered furniture. On the dusty windowsill were numerous gifts—books, pots of wilted flowers, unopened boxes of candy. On the aluminum typing table were untidy piles of manuscripts and a battered old manual typewriter and, on a hospital tray, a glass pitcher one-third filled with fruit juice and several small paper cups that had the look of having been used. Belatedly H. invited his visitors to sit and asked would they like a drink?—pouring fruit juice into the cups and handing them over before either could decline. Thank you, they murmured awkwardly, but when neither could bring himself to sip from his cup H. seized the wrist of the man nearest him, leaned over, and spat into the liquid. Now you know why you don't want any of my grapefruit juice! he said laughingly.

They all laughed, relieved. It was the old H. after all.

Visitors to Building E were allowed only forty-five minutes. The remainder of the time passed pleasantly if rather slowly: H. insisted upon hearing news, gossip—who of their old friends was where and with whom and for how long and what had become of and did they know anything further of—but paid little attention to details, chuckling, and murmuring from time to time with an air of deep satisfaction, Yes! Of course! When it was time for his visitors to leave they rose shakily to their feet, their limbs strangely heavy, their eyeballs seared in their sockets as if they'd been staring into a blinding light. H. heaved himself up from his chair in a well-practiced maneuver—on the whole, H. was shorter than they recalled but heavier, almost massive about the shoulders and torso—and locked them in bearlike hugs, each in turn. How strong he was, still! So close, the odor of disinfectant made their eyes water; his bristling gray hair scratched like wires against their cheeks.

H. wore an attractive quilted robe and bedroom slippers; flashes of his white bare legs suggested that he no longer had ankles, and that his legs were hairless as a child's. Yet he seemed, for the moment at least, jolly enough.

Wagging his finger he said, I know when I'll see you boys again!

They did not ask when he thought he would see them again.

At the end of the long empty corridor they paused to look back and sure enough their friend stood swaying in the doorway of his room, grinning and waving.

No nurses or attendants were in sight. The young black man in the entry had disappeared. In their agitation they couldn't remember how to operate the motorized vehicle and after several vexed, frustrating minutes they decided, despite their exhaustion, and the considerable distance to the front gate, that they would walk.

The Maker of Parables

M., the maker of parables, a small dwarfish delicately built man with shining dark eyes, lived inside a large slovenly bearlike man of late middle age. Each morning the two clambered up out of sleep, the one trembling with anticipation to set down, in the crystalline prose for which, while yet living, he had become immortal, the beautiful and terrifying wisdom yielded him by night; the other trembling with anticipation to eat—to eat, and eat, and eat. For there was a ravenous hole in his belly.

There was then each morning of M.'s life, unknown to his admirers, this struggle between *words* demanding to be recorded—for words are perishable as those who utter them—and *appetite:* the big slovenly fellow seating himself with a sigh of contentment to eat, and eat, and eat. Eating, he was at peace. He and his destiny were one, not even the thinness of a shadow between them. And afterward he drifted in a dream like that of an infant in the womb.

Then for a certain privileged space of time M. was free to write. He wrote quickly, furiously, scarcely daring to pause, for fear the other would wake suddenly to fresh pangs of appetite; and his precious freedom would be curtailed. Thus is a maker of parables a desperate man: his little stories, rarely more than one or two pages, are exclusively of desperation.

Icy cold and passionless, the parables, fed by appetite, disdain all knowledge of appetite; or of the large slovenly bearlike fellow whose laboring jaws make them possible. The maker of parables, M., contemplating the mirror's gross reflection, cannot see himself in it: this, he calls his destiny.

His admirers would not have it otherwise.

Embrace

One day, quietly, with no warning, she said, "Will you hold me?"

And so he did, of course. His arms around her in an embrace that fitted his body to hers. Kissing her hair, eyelids, tip of nose. Asking, "Did something go wrong? Did you have a scare?"

She seemed not to have heard, her arms around him tight, tight.

Feeling against her cheek the comforting scratchiness of the wool sweater she'd knitted him years ago. When they were newly lovers.

Minutes passed. How very odd. He felt her trembling—a deep subterranean shuddering. He asked, "You didn't have an accident with your car, did you?" And, "Did someone threaten you?" And, "What *is* it?"

Still she made no reply. Gripping him close.

So he was having difficulty breathing. So his heartbeat quickened, as if in the presence of danger.

He said, "Darling, please, I love you—what *is* it?"

He tried gently to push her away from him, just a bit, so that he could see her face. For, suddenly, it seemed to him he could not recall her face.

But she was holding him tight, tight.

Saying, almost inaudibly, so that he felt rather than heard her words, "Just hold me."

"Yes, but—what *is* it?"

How many minutes of this embrace could he endure?—five?—ten? Sixty? One thousand? He said, bravely, "Yes. I'm here."

Outside, an unexpected rain pelted against the windows—or was that sunshine? That sudden glare?

Beauty Salon

He must have passed the nondescript little neighborhood beauty salon countless times without so much as glancing at it and certainly without being struck by its weatherworn, feebly glamorous sign—*LA JOLIE BEAUTY SALON "Unisex" Hair Styling*—or pausing to consider the melancholy meanings layered beneath the primary, pragmatic meaning of "unisex"; but now on this gusty white day, a day of windblown clouds and flying grit, he found himself stopped dead on the sidewalk thinking, why not?

It was that kind of day. The wind must have had something to do with it. You could kill yourself, or go for a long walk until you staggered with fatigue, or decide impulsively to have your hair "styled."

So without giving himself time to change his mind he entered the La Jolie Salon.

How different the atmosphere was from that of the gentlemen's barbershop in the city's best hotel, to which he'd gone for twenty-odd years—here, commingled with the familiar, sweetly cloying odors of shampoo, hair lotion, oils, cologne or perfume, was a sharp chemical odor that pinched his nostrils: permanent wave set, he supposed. It smelled like formaldehyde.

And the decor was conspicuously feminine—the slightly shabby wallpaper a velvety gold embossed with black arabesques, mirrored panels on all sides, a vase of wilted pink and orange gladioli on the receptionist's counter.

156

And not a man in sight.

Not many customers at all, in fact.

There were only three chairs; two sinks for shampooing; a row of eight or ten hair dryers in an alcove to the rear. The shop was hardly larger than a single room of average proportions, a living room for instance, and judging by the startled glances he drew—from the two beauty operators on the floor and from one of their customers, an elderly woman whose white hair was being wound on tiny rollers—he had blundered by coming in.

But he did not retreat. It was that kind of day—you improvised, and discovered later what you'd meant.

In any case he had nowhere else to go.

One of the beauty operators was a woman in her fifties, solid, busty, in orthopedic-looking shoes, with a face creased as if she'd spent too much time in the sun, the other was a short slender girl in her mid-twenties perhaps, striking, glamorous in an outmoded Liz Taylor style, hair too black not to be dyed, enormous sunburst earrings, long fingernails, intricately made-up face. Both had customers and there seemed to be no one on duty at the receptionist's counter and he found himself willing that the elder of the two would come to him, if either elected to come, since he had grown to resist contemplating, let alone considering, attractive young women; he didn't want his senses stirred.

After a moment the younger beauty operator came over, "Yes? Do you have an appointment, sir?" making an effort to smile though clearly vexed. She must have known he didn't have an appointment. He said defensively, indicating a sign in the front window, "—I didn't think an appointment was necessary."

The girl said, "Depends." She was frowning at the appointments ledger open on the counter. Inside the coarse makeup mask the girl's features were delicate but her stance was adult, subtly resistant. Her eyelashes were stiff and black as a spider's legs, her curved eyebrows looked crayoned, her moist, glossily red lips matched her talon-like fingernails. A badge on the left breast of her gold-and-black striped smock read *Veronica*.

Sighing she asked what did he want done and he told her humbly enough and she stared pointedly at the clock on the wall—an extravagant sunburst design, like her earrings—and said, "All right mister I'll do you soon as I finish my comb-out, that'll be maybe five minutes if you'd like to be seated?" So he said yes, thank you, good, suddenly weak with gratitude, as if a danger had been forestalled.

He didn't at all mind waiting if there was a purpose to the waiting. This was a phase of his life when, not in the active grip of anxiety, he didn't at all mind waiting.

He took off his cashmere overcoat and Tartan-plaid muffler and hung them neatly on a peg on the wall; sat in a vinyl chair rather uncomfortably near a young mother in jeans and mud-splattered boots with a fretting baby; leafed through magazines as he waited. He felt conspicuous, something of a fool, knowing everyone in the shop—operators, customers—was well aware of him, and if not whispering about him, prepared to do so. If he glanced up he would see eyes affixed to him by way of mirrors but he resolved not to be intimidated, for why did the shop advertise its services for both women and men—indeed, there were posters of male models too on the walls—if the presence of a man so surprised them? Had he come here as a young man in his thirties, as the man he'd been then, what would they have made of him!

The beauty operators and their customers were chatting together companionably, a rambling female music he found mysterious and intriguing. But he did not want to overhear. He did not want to feel envy. He leafed through hair styling magazines examining photographs of male models with a consumer's critical eye, as if it were within his power to pick and choose which "look" he wanted. Here and there amid the glossy pages of stridently attractive young men and women there were older men and women, silvery-haired, white-haired, yet not, if one looked closely, really old; not old in the ways that counted, the ways that could not be disguised. "Older" in this context meant, say, fifty-five at the most. He did not resent it, he'd grown accustomed to it this past decade, the shifting of the world's attention from him not as a personality—for of course he retained his *person*—but as a physical presence, a body amid a contention of other bodies. Where once women looked at him and their eyes might look in interest, curiosity, outright attraction, now they did not see him at all, simply looked through him as if he were not there or were standing between them and the true object of their attentions. Yet it was worse for women, he supposed. Always worse for women. His wives had suffered that sort of injustice and he had been able to sympathize with them while detaching himself from them. The hurt he'd caused had hurt him too but had not for that reason altered the course of his life.

Selfish, they'd called him.

Cruel. Cold-hearted.

And yes, yes he supposed it was true, he could not deny it must seem true, to others though never to himself. I am the person I am, he thought. The mild shaking of his hand made the glossy magazine pages ripple as he turned them.

He found himself staring at photographs in one of the more exotic of the magazines—punk, waxed, dyed, corn-rowed, Afro, teased, puffed, braided hair styles. Most of the male models wore gold studs in their ears, some of them several studs.

At last—it was far more than five minutes—Veronica came to fetch him. Her manner was both sullen and accommodating as if, even in a bad mood, she were obliged to be courteous to her elders. He noted that she wore shoes with heels, though she must be on her feet all day. And those amazing fingernails—how could she do her job without breaking them?

She seated him ceremonially in a reclining chair before one of the sinks; draped a slightly soiled plastic cape over his shoulders; briskly turned on the water. She cranked the chair back and as he was lowered, the base of his skull brought to rest against the hard rim of the sink, he felt a touch of vertigo—almost of fear. What did this remind him of? Of what was he thinking?

Belatedly, he removed his glasses and held them clutched in his lap.

"You like it hot, or what?" Veronica asked. "Or don't mind?"

She smelled of sweet perfume, or of hair spray, or was it chewing gum?—he noticed to his disappointment that she was chewing gum, in slow, idle, then abruptly rapid rhythms, as if in pace with her thoughts.

Shyly, he shut his eyes as she shampooed his hair. He could have wished his hair were thicker, as it had once been; though, for a man of his age . . . Despite her long sharp fingernails Veronica had no apparent difficulty washing his hair, massaging the scalp. He quite liked it, the hard canny fingers of a woman unknown to him.

But he did not like it that, on all sides, the women's chatter continued. There were exclamations, there were fits of laughter. They spoke of someone known to them who had just had her fourth baby; of someone's husband who had "totaled" his new car; of a customer who had come in the other day for a perm—"I didn't think she looked exactly right, sort of puffy-faced," Veronica said in an aggrieved voice, "but anyway I gave her the perm, and under the dryer it went all matted. She hadn't said a word about having chemotherapy treatments, which she should have done—I could have predicted that would happen." She paused; the others plied her with questions. "She's wearing a wig now," Veronica concluded. "She should have known better I guess, but you can't blame them."

She gave him a second shampoo and a second rinse; asked him did he want any conditioner; then with a mother's rough yet seemingly affectionate touch she toweled the moisture out of his hair and led him to one of the swivel chairs. Trailing the dripping cape, a bit blind without his glasses, he felt awkward, womanish. In the big facing mirror his reflection floated like something decomposing in water. Beside him Veronica's reflection, the gaudy stripes of her smock, took on an emphatic solidity.

But Veronica seemed more kindly disposed to him now. Perhaps she was developing a professional interest in him, as a problem to be solved.

Briskly she combed his hair with a long-handled metal comb, removing hairs and flicking them from her fingers with no expression he could discern of distaste or of concern at how much of his hair did indeed come out after a shampoo. He saw the gleam of rings on her slender hands, the fluid airborne red of her long fingernails. He breathed in the acrid, eye-watering smell of chemical—the heavyset middle-aged woman in the chair beside him was having a permanent wave: a timer close by clicked off the minutes—until, as it mixed with Veronica's sweet moist powdery smell, he scarcely noticed. Veronica asked him how he wanted his hair done?—how short at the front, the sides, the back?—had he maybe found a style that suited him in one of the styling magazines? He was embarrassed to realize that she'd noticed him looking through the magazines. Curtly he said, "No. I'll leave it to your judgment."

Veronica was wary; she must have had experience with customers who, having eschewed personal responsibility, later blamed her for their disappointment. She brought over one of the magazines and opened it to a page of older gentlemen—of course: "Something like this, maybe?" He laughed, his face reddening, and agreed. The absurdity of the situation, its vanity and pathos, seemed not to strike Veronica.

But then it was her business of course. Like any professional whose service is the human body in one or another of its needs.

So Veronica began trimming his hair, humming to herself, rapt in concentration. The snick! snick! snick! of the scissors made him tense involuntarily. Tiny hairs got into his eyes, down inside his collar. He'd replaced his glasses so that he could see but he did not choose to see, so bluntly before him, his own image in the mirror; he preferred to watch Veronica's.

He was amused by her working-class glamour, her Cleopatra eyes and eyebrows, her fussily arranged synthetic-looking black hair. And the gleaming red fingernails, the longest nearly two inches, rather repulsive to see. Yet he heard himself say sincerely, "How do you get your fingernails to grow so long?—so long and beautiful?"

The word "beautiful" leapt strangely from his tongue. He hoped it would not alarm or annoy Veronica but she only laughed, flattered, and murmured that they weren't all hers exactly—"These here are my own," she said, brandishing two or three of the talons close by his face, "—and these are sculpted." Seeing his blank look she said, "You know—fake. We do them here, actually. My girl friend and me, we do each other."

"But don't they break off easily?"

Veronica shrugged, snipping away at his hair. Gunmetal gray wisps drifted past his eyes, caught on the lenses of his glasses. "If they do," she said matter-of-factly, "there's plenty more where they came from."

The telephone rang at the receptionist's counter. The other operator had drifted off so Veronica answered it. Her telephone manner was relaxed, cordial, perfunctory. As soon as she hung up the telephone rang again and this time it seemed to be a personal call; as if she'd forgotten her gentleman customer sitting patiently in his chair, face slightly flushed, glasses catching the light, she laughed and chatted for some minutes. He gathered she was talking with a woman friend, someone whose children played with hers. So she was married . . . but of course she would be married. He tried not to eavesdrop on her conversation but found himself listening eagerly. A wave of envy like nausea stirred in his bowels.

When she returned he said as if casually, " 'Veronica'—that's a saint's name, you know." When she did not respond, not even to glance at him in the mirror, he said, trying very hard not to sound pedantic or old-mannish, "—St. Veronica gave a handkerchief to Christ on the cross, and the imprint of his face remained on the handkerchief. Or so legend has it."

Veronica laughed, coloring pleasantly. She said, "Well—that was a long time ago." She paused and added, as if to rebuff any attempt at flattery, "Also, I didn't name myself."

"It's a beautiful name though. 'Veronica.' "

"It just gets shortened to 'Ronnie.' "

"Is that what they call you?—'Ronnie'?"

She shrugged again, stooping over his head. The scissors and metal comb flashed expertly. He said, "What is your last name?" without intending quite to ask and Veronica finessed the question by seeming not to hear and at the same time asking one of her own about whether he'd ever had his hair styled before. It had grown out so uneven, she said, she couldn't tell.

"No," he said. "I don't believe I have. Not 'styled' exactly."

The haircut was going by too quickly. In a few minutes he would be expelled to the street.

Anxious to make conversation, to engage her attention, he asked if she was married? If she had children?—and Veronica smiled again with pleasure and pointed out a row of color snapshots affixed to the mirror. "That's Johnny, he's six, and that's Timmy, he's two. That's me with Timmy, just home from the hospital. That's all of us and my mother too, last summer at Harburton Park. You know

that Park?'' He squinted at these snapshots of strangers. Wistfully
he said, "You seem so young to have a six-year-old." Veronica made
a childish snorting noise as if she believed herself teased. "I'm older
than I look, maybe," she said.

Pointlessly he joked, "Well—so am I."

Veronica tactfully overlooked the joke. She finished trimming his
hair, shook strands and wisps and stray hairs away from his shoulders, rubbed a fragrant coconut-smelling cream on her hands and
then briskly over his head. Again, with a sensation almost of pain,
he wished his hair were thicker, his scalp less exposed. He persisted, "You hardly look twenty!" in a tone of avuncular reproach,
wondering at once why on earth he said such a thing, why, knowing
better, he was drifting into aimless banter, flirtation. This self-
assured young woman in the prime of her physical being—her
hardy beauty, her sexuality—could have no other feeling for him
than pity, if it came to that.

He was thinking how slow it was to die, the terrible need to be
liked; to be admired, respected, *seen*. If only in the eyes of these
anonymous others, to be *seen*.

He asked if many of the salon's customers requested the more
avant-garde hair styles. Veronica said, "Oh no—not here. This is
sort of just, you know, a neighborhood place, mainly local customers. We don't do much high style."

Her voice trailed off, it seemed, wistfully. He asked, "Would you
rather work somewhere else?"

Quickly she said, "Oh no, I'm happy here."

The older beauty operator was out of earshot. He said as if con-
spiratorially, "I suppose other, newer beauty salons are more—"

"—yes, right, if you want really high style—"

"—like downtown? In the Hilton—?"

"And out in the new shopping mall—"

"And the clientele, and the tips—"

"There's just more going on," Veronica said, nodding, meeting
his eye in the mirror, "—places like that. But like I said, I'm happy
here, I've been here five years. Lots of my mom's friends are my
customers."

"You're close to your mother, Veronica?"

She blinked at him, vaguely smiling. "You mean where I live, or in my heart?"

"Oh—either!" he said, struck by her quaint expression, "—or both."

Now, as if at last he'd said something truly witty, or truly charming, she flashed him a dazzling smile by way of the mirror. She liked him, suddenly. She said happily, "I guess both."

Next she took up a hand dryer, turning it gracefully in her left hand while with her right, using an oddly shaped comb—like a Spanish comb, but metallic—she lifted and smoothed and "shaped" his lank, damp hair as if trying to cajole it into thickness and body. At first he could not watch—the effort seemed so hopeless. Nor did he care to see the gravely neutral expression on his face, the pursing of his lips, the dark, seemingly dilated nostrils, the eyes shy and hopeful behind the bifocal lenses. Confronted with his image in a mirrored surface when he wasn't prepared for it his instinct was to recoil: that isn't me. In truth he'd grown into a dignified and even fairly attractive older man, in the miasma of his sixties, poised as if visibly between late middle age and the uncharted and irrefutable wilderness of true old age. Yet—that isn't me! None of you know who I am!

Suddenly he heard himself say, "I haven't been well. This is my first day—I mean, my first fairly normal day—out. I had surgery six weeks ago." Immediately he wondered why he'd told a stranger something so intimate; so, in its way, shameful.

Veronica's face crinkled in quick sympathy. But her tone was wary—"Oh that's too bad."

He felt his cheeks redden. His heart kicked sullen and hurtful in his chest. Having initiated the subject he could not simply drop it. He said, smiling, making an airy gesture that lifted the plastic cape awkwardly, "Oh no—not at all. The operation was quite successful. More like a surgical procedure than an actual operation . . . " Why was he saying so much? Had a switch been pulled? He was a man of so few words otherwise, and these words so carefully, almost grudgingly chosen, what was happening to him now? He forced himself to be still, though his smile persisted—a hopeful tic of a smile which Veronica chose to ignore. He stared into the mirror as the young woman with her monstrously frizzed and plaited black hair and her pouty red lips labored at styling his hair, frowning in concentration. Her task in his case must be a particularly challenging one.

What, he wondered, would she think if she knew that he had a bit of money and, in certain quarters, a bit of "reputation"?—would it make any difference? And if she knew that in his heart he felt himself superior, as if by the privilege of birth itself, to this tacky little beauty salon and everyone and everything connected with it? Would it make any difference?

He whispered, "I don't want to die, I'm not ready."

If canny Veronica heard these words she gave no sign. The discreet humming of the hand dryer's motor had probably drowned them out.

"Well—how do you like it, sir?"

The smiling beauty operator was holding a hand mirror so that, in his vanity, he might examine his newly styled hair, indeed his newly styled head, from the sides and back. The leprous bald spot in the back had not been disguised but its exact dimensions were ingeniously obscured. The hair itself—dull, limp, gunmetal-gray that morning—now shone, even glared, with evident health; indeed, it gave an impression of being magically sculpted, every strand stiffly in place. "It's—very fine," he said, staring. He did not know whether to be transfixed by his image or simply embarrassed. How had the ministrations of mere scissors, comb, hand dryer, and hair oil worked such a transformation? His skin had acquired a pleasant flush as if lightly sunburnt and his eyes were a mariner's blue. "It's very fine," he repeated. With wondering fingers he touched the sides and, shyly, the silvery bar of hair that curved above his forehead from left to right; that so flattering, so startling change in his appearance. Where had his part gone? Was there no longer any part? How on earth would he comb this outlandish hair, by himself?

As if accidentally, in appeal, he touched Veronica's hand holding the mirror; and seemingly without calculation too she drew away in an utterly natural, unhurried gesture.

Veronica was girlishly pleased with her work. "How do you like it?" she asked again, hands on her hips. He said, untangling himself from the cape and getting to his feet, elation like a balloon swelling his heart, "I like it very much, Veronica. Thank you."

"Molly come look!" Veronica cried, and to his annoyance the other operator came to examine the modest transformation that had been executed, lavish with praise, well-intentioned flattery. He couldn't help but laugh, his face warming: it was all so foolish, so embarrassing. But one had to be a good sport. He had no doubt but that the two women were wholly sincere in the extravagances they uttered, and not condescending, or patronizing, or mocking. That was hardly the way of a neighborhood beauty salon.

Happy Veronica touched his sleeve. "I *told* you you'd like this style, sir, didn't I?"

"Oh yes," he said, happy too at being on the verge of being teased, as if by a frisky niece. "Yes you did."

He'd forgotten what words if any he had uttered while the hand dryer had hummed in his ears.

He only knew he must never come back.

Now it was time to pay. Luckily the receptionist had never appeared; perhaps, weekday mornings in so becalmed an establishment, no receptionist was needed. Veronica manned the antiquated cash register herself, chewing gum snappily, chatting with him about the weather, the damned wind, the delay in spring—"I complain to my husband, 'Where's spring?' and he says, smart guy, 'Honey this *is* spring: check the calendar.' "

She added up the bill, including tax, and it came to a little more than he would have expected in so modest a place. But of course he paid her without hesitation; and discreetly slipped a folded bill into her hand as a tip. At first she smiled, as if surprised; suddenly a bit shy; then, seeing the bill's denomination, she simply stared; stopped smiling. "Just to show my regard," he said quickly.

Fumblingly he buttoned his overcoat; wound his muffler around his neck; was eager to be gone. He feared he had violated the young woman's dignity and he did not want to observe her face, to note how pride and desire might there contend; it seemed to him ungentlemanly, like scrutinizing a lover's face at the moment of orgasm.

So he left, quickly. Stepped out onto the sidewalk, began to walk away. But an instant later Veronica followed, calling, "Mister? Mister, wait!"

His heart pounded violently. "Yes?"

"I guess you made a mistake? Gave me too much?" She ran up to him, her hair billowing in the wind, her gummed-up eyes narrowed. She held the bill up prominently. He said quickly, "Oh no—it isn't a mistake." She said, "Yes, well, but it sort of *is*—you'd better take it back." He said, hurt, "Why? Why take it back? It's for you." She said, "I can't accept this—I don't accept tips." He said, "You don't accept tips?" Half-angrily she said, "No sir I don't." She was regarding him critically, standing rather close; as if unable to decide whether he was a friend or an enemy. "It's—it's just my way."

He thought, You're lying.

She held the bill out to him and he refused to take it.

Annoyed, puzzled, laughing like a frustrated child, she tried to shove the bill into his overcoat pocket—but he blocked her.

"Hey mister please: take it back," she said. "No," he said, "it's yours." "I don't accept tips, I told you," she said. "Certainly you do," he said. "I told you I don't!" she said. "Then don't think of it as a tip," he said. So like lovers they quarreled on the sidewalk as the wind tore at them, whipping their hair.

Abandoned

If this is going to upset you, he said, we shouldn't stop. But she was already getting out of the car.

This was devastation. This was shame, insult. Here was, not the green she remembered, or, in winter, the dazzling white slopes of snow, but a place of dereliction—the asphalt paths cracked and weedy, the benches broken, graffiti-covered, grass crudely mowed, not even raked, and left to burn out in the summer heat. And something further: had the park shrunken? was it literally smaller?

It was a city park comprised of a number of hills and in the waning afternoon light patches of straw on the facing hills caught the light like flame.

A pulse beat angrily in her head. Forty years!

Her husband was maneuvering their car into a parking place on the street. She turned away, impatient. She didn't want him to walk with her, didn't want to be expected to speak.

They'd been married twenty-five years. They were not sentimental people. Sometimes they observed each other as if through the wrong end of a telescope, seeing images that were coolly reduced, negotiable.

Once, she'd ice-skated in this park. Fort Lee Historic Park, on the Palisades Parkway. Her father had taught her. He'd been patient, loving. She had seen him only up close, magnified. But he'd been a big man, too. She was certain. She didn't need old snapshots, to judge.

Where did you go? Why?

It was the winter before the spring of his death that her father had taught her to ice-skate here. She could remember vividly the steely glint of the ice, the shock of its hardness when she fell. The squeals and shouts of small children like herself, the rink that was so enormous, intimidating, sunk deep inside what must have been a glacial hollow in the earth, its sides nearly symmetrical; a strangeness to it, as if it were a stage observed from a high balcony. And the steps Daddy had led her down so cautiously, not real steps but lengths of log set in the earth, slick and treacherous with ice, and Daddy gripped her mittened hand tight, and she had skates that smelled of newness, white leather shoes set atop perfect steel blades, and there was laughter between them quick and perishable as their breaths, and she was happy. Her eyes smarting with tears in the cold wind, her cheeks burning with excitement, an almost unbearable excitement, her ankles weak, the bones like water, and there was her tall smiling father executing maneuvers on the ice to astonish her—then skating to her, backward, so easily! Like magic.

She'd stared. She'd been eight, that winter. That would be Daddy's last winter.

The snowy hills and the ice rink and the happy amplified music and the crowd of skaters, she remembered. But she didn't really remember the girl with the skates, the girl wiping her nose on her redmittened hand, nor the man who was Daddy, the man soon to die, leading her out onto the ice with whispered words of encouragement, steadying her on the shaky skates.

Now she entered the park, in summer. Like a sleepwalker, entering it. She was relieved to think that, since it was summer, the old skating rink would be a children's wading pool. And wasn't there a fountain at its center out of which spouted gay gushing sparkling water, water like flame, high into the air? You stared and stared unable to look away.

It was June now by the calendar but already the grass was burnt out. There was a fierce, blinding early evening sun alternating with splotches of shadow, gusts of actual chill. Storm clouds like Novem-

ber had been following them in the car for hours, a wearing, hyp-
notic drive down from Maine, hours in the car and another long
stretch before they would be home.

Her hair was whipping in the wind. A hot, powerful wind blowing up dirt and bits of straw into her face.

He called after her words she didn't quite hear, and made no
effort to hear. She called back, cupping her hands against the wind,
I'm all right! Please just leave me alone.

Over twenty-five years they'd grown to love each other the way
twins love each other. Without being required to see each other.

The park actually *was* smaller, she hadn't imagined it: a wooded
area that had once faced the street, presumably public land, was
gone, and in its place an apartment building of about thirty stories
had been erected. This struck her as outrageous. Public land? Sold?

The greater mystery was why, at this time of day, in this season
of the year, was the park nearly empty? Had it become a dangerous
place? Shivering, she heard the wind stirring the parched grasses,
the dried husks of things rattling in the trees. It was the future, was
it? The year 3000. Everyone had died. Beyond the fat dimpled
rainclouds the sky was the color of faintly bloodied gauze. In another minute she would begin to scream.

Those years, she'd been a good, sweet child. Quiet. Obedient.

She didn't remember, really. But she'd been told this was so.

When Daddy died, never came home but was taken to a hospital
from his office, a place where, before even her mother had gotten
there, he had died, things came to a stop—a full stop.

Then started again, a little later. She couldn't have said how
much later.

They'd moved away from Fort Lee, Mommy and her, there was
a day of men who came to pack: wrapping dishware in special paper,
setting things in deep packing cartons, lamps stripped of their
shades looking strange, skeletal, bedsprings exposed like something
you aren't meant to see. The new address, memorized forever, was
131 West 78th Street, New York City. In time, at that address,
there would be a new father, a new happiness. Not Daddy, but a
new father, and a new happiness. A baby brother, and a second baby
brother. That's how it is. You must know that's how it is.

· · ·

The old skating rink was not visible from this path. She told herself there was no necessity she seek it out: why expose yourself to hurt? tears? Why, when you are nearly fifty years old, and have forgotten so much?

Instead, she found herself staring at four figures on a nearby hill. They were vividly colored as swabs of paint and charged with meaning as figures in an El Greco painting, if only you could grasp the meaning. Two policemen questioning a Hispanic man and a young woman pushing a baby stroller in the direction of the men, slowly.

The policemen's uniforms—short-sleeved shirts, trousers—were an intense blue. The woman's shift was a bright shimmering yellow. The Hispanic man's gesturing hands, hands of pleading, moved seemingly of their own volition.

Something had happened. Or would shortly happen. She shivered, not wanting to know.

Still she was not looking back toward her husband, she was walking swiftly along the cracked, weedy path. She was thinking, Maybe none of this is real. The park was neglected as an old graveyard.

She wanted to hold on to her anger. To keep from feeling something else.

The skates had been a Christmas present like nothing before or since. Certainly, nothing since. Unwrapping the red crinkling paper, her breath in short spurts . . . soft white leather and lovely steel blades and the white laces Daddy would tie for her, Sundays, his breath steaming, squatting in front of her as she sat on a park bench, her legs too short for her feet to touch the ground. And then round and round in wild hilarious shrieking circles on the ice. Daddy! Daddy!—as the world shifted from under her and she fell.

This is what frightens: the tales the brain tells. Behind the wheel of a speeding car, for instance. In moments of excruciating intimacy, for instance. Never does it cease, not even when you sleep. And when you die?

She looked quickly over her shoulder, shading her eyes. Her husband was strolling some distance behind her, at his own unhurried pace. No urgency to his limbs, no need to constrain or comfort her, he was a strong, stubborn man, a man given to periods of silence, a man who didn't insist. Now he sat on one of the rotted benches, taking care it didn't break beneath his weight. He stretched his legs, he was content. The other too sometimes sat like that, here in the park. On that same bench, perhaps.

She thought, There is nothing that can't be forgotten.

Don't do it, she thought. Even as she was making her way down the rotted steps, to the ruin below.

This was what remained of the old skating rink, the children's pool in summer. Here, on the rim of the hill, the wind was even fiercer, tearing at her hair, her clothes. Whipping her skirt against her legs. There was no water in the pool, of course, you would hardly identify it as a pool, just a concrete oval in the earth, discolored, abandoned. Even the fountain had been removed. It was just cracked concrete sunken six inches below ground level, much smaller than she recalled. A look of antiquity. The parched surface of a dead planet.

She stared, in wonder. Her cheeks were damp, the wind had made her eyes tear.

Still, it can interest you as an aesthetic phenomenon. The way in which the cracked and buckling concrete seemed to have broken along precise fissure lines, forming rectangles of almost identical sizes, approximately three feet square, bordered by dun-colored, dying weeds, in patterns almost geometrical. You could see it as beautiful, if you tried.

Especially at this hour of the day. The sun waning, sepia, yielding to dusk.

Down in the hollow, the wind was less severe.

She walked slowly along the ledge of the old rink, the old wading pool. Slowly. She wasn't thinking of anything, really. She was not a sentimental woman.

Mmmmm hey lady!—a voice sounded from above.

She glanced up startled to see a boy at the crest of the hill, at the top of the very steps she'd taken down. He was watching her. He was squatting, heavy thighs straining the fabric of his jeans. Hey lady! Hiya! Watcha doin'! he cried. There was a mirthful mockery to his voice.

For some seconds she stared up at him, and he stared down at her. He was grinning broadly. His muscled shoulders were hunched, his fingers circling teasingly at his groin. He wore an undershirt that fitted him tightly. He might have been about fifteen, a white boy, but his skin gray, his mouth damp and slack. His flat-topped hair was the color of broom sage.

When she returned to the car where her husband was waiting, her face had recomposed itself. But must have been pale, waxen. The edges of her mouth must have been white. Her husband, seeing, took her cold hands in his and squeezed them and said, gently, but reprovingly, You look as if you've just come back from a long distance. Quickly she smiled, and said, No, you don't understand, I was never away.

Running

Here is what happened. Except, of course, nothing happened.

Their third day out, they went running along a hiking trail beside Lake Mt. Moriah in the northeastern corner of the Adirondack Forest Preserve, running at a moderate speed, not pushing themselves, for they were not serious or obsessed runners, not marathon runners, neither in fact had been athletic or much interested in competitive sports in adolescence, she a slender dark-haired woman in her early thirties, he a tall, big-boned silvery-blond man a few years older, and she was running ahead since the trail was too narrow for them to run comfortably side by side, and he had to stop to retie a shoelace, he murmured, "Damn!" though good-naturedly, for he was a good-natured man, and she ran on, retaining her speed, she was in excellent spirits, as she often was at such times, sacred times they seemed to her, the ease of running, the childlike pleasure, the illusion of being weightless, bodiless, without a name, as if, only at such moments, the physical being propelled through space, the soul, assuming there is a soul, defines itself *This is happiness!—my truest self*, and she was relieved that the sky had cleared, no rain clouds, it was a windy sunny brightly cool August morning, a day of aching beauty, the previous day they'd driven too long and much of the time in pelting rain, in close confinement in the car that, while technically his, they shared for ambitious drives, so the mere fact of a clear sky was a simple fact of happiness, she

was one to be grateful for such things, and the sharp fragrance of the
pine needles underfoot, and Lake Mt. Moriah, one of the region's
numerous glacier lakes, that, the evening before, checking into
their motel, they'd hardly been able to make out in the dusk, was
so luminous as to seem unreal, a lake out of a dream, reflecting as
in a polished metallic surface the sculpted sky and the dark serrated
rim of trees, evergreens, birches, that surrounded it, she felt the
blood beating hard and exuberant in her veins—*I can do anything!
I need no one!*—and turning a corner she emerged into a grassy
clearing of boulders, gigantic boulders that looked as if they were
pushing up from the earth, covered with lichen, lichen like a man's
beard, and deeply creased, like human faces compressed and dis-
torted, and the wind in the topmost branches of trees was visible
here, the effort, the seeming emotion, the trail divided into a broad,
not very clearly defined V, the left branch curving back to the lake
in the deep shadow of evergreens and the right branch, beyond
several more boulders, into an unexpected meadow of tall grasses,
Queen Anne's lace, milkweed gone to seed, dazzling goldenrod—
How beautiful: and if no one saw it!—and she seemed not to
hesitate, not even for a fraction of a second, it was as if gravity drew
her to the right branch of the trail, and away from the lake, she was
not thinking *How will he know which way I've gone,* nor was she
thinking *Will he be puzzled, concerned, not knowing which way
I've gone?* for she was a woman of moods and impulses and spon-
taneity, that was one of the ways in which, in the human world, she
defined herself, and was defined, and she was curious, following the
trail upward through the meadow, wondering where it would lead,
guessing that, shortly, it would loop back to the lake, if it did not,
and he didn't seem to be following her, she would turn back, return
to the lakeshore trail, catch up with him from behind, as she sometimes did she would surprise him, playfully approaching him from
behind—*Here I am! Did you wonder where I was?*—she was beginning to sweat inside her clothes, her khaki shorts, loose-fitting
white shirt, a gauzy maroon-orange scarf tying her hair back from
her face, but it was a good feeling, yes and the mild ache of her
muscles, the calm hard defiant beat of her heart, she was thinking
with pleasure too of returning to the motel room and showering and

they would have their late breakfast, the routines of their lives together were comforting, yes, but they were confining, too, predictable and confining—*Are we addicted? To what are we addicted?*—thinking that they were a couple well matched, companionable, not married though they had been together for nearly four years and though they lived, at least much of the time (as on this eight-day drive through the Adirondacks, for instance: but often they traveled separately) as if they were married, yes, and married for years, casual acquaintances assumed they were a married couple, for there was between them an unstudied ease, a companionable cheerfulness, a manner suggesting familiar marital customs exercised without self-consciousness, or much emotion, they were professional people, she an administrator for a public school district, he an engineer at one of the Bell Laboratories, yes, but she wanted to return to graduate school to get another degree, in comparative literature, perhaps, and he was in his heart a purely theoretical mathematician, she was thinking of how strange it was, how simple a fact yet how strange, that he was the man who loved her and whom of all men she loved, how strange that they might be defined in that way, and, in another era, her mother's era, for instance, they would be married, would have married years ago, would have children, a child, at least, and if so who would that child be, for she had had an abortion once, and this was a secret from him, this was always to be a secret from him, as from her family, she told herself, *It matters to no one if it doesn't matter to me: and it doesn't matter to me,* and in truth she rarely thought of it, she never thought of it, she was not that terrified girl of nineteen, though terror surfaced in her sometimes, not that terror but another, she did not believe there was any connection, the girl of nineteen was vanished, forgotten, she could not remember the boy's face (and he was not a man, but a boy: her own age), but she knew she had not loved him, or, if she had loved him, it had been a mistake, just as, perhaps, the love she felt for the man who was not her husband was a mistake, a sickness of a kind, a sickness that had no name, because she feared losing him, he who was so good-natured, so kindly, so loyal a friend, a man of temperate desires and ambitions, a man so reliable, having no idea of the hunger she felt

for him, her secret terror of being left by him, her terror even that
he should know, should even suspect, though he was a man without suspicion, that she did fear losing him, that, sometimes, the
terror woke her from sleep, her heart pounding erratically, a taste of
something brackish at the back of her mouth while beside her,
unknowing, the man who was not her husband slept his heavy,
healthy sleep, drawing his deep rhythmic breaths undisturbed, yes,
and had not one of her dream terrors wakened her only a few
mornings ago, back in the city, the anticipation of this trip into the
mountains, perhaps, had dislodged the terror, but of course she hid
it from him, she shared everything with him by day, but really she
shared very little with him, this too he did not know, he could not
guess how by day, especially when she was running, she felt angry
contempt for that other woman, that sick woman, that coward who
was, yet was not, herself, for she was a wholly free agent, a woman
with a career, an only moderately paying career but a career nonetheless, and hers, she was economically independent of any man, as
her mother, and her mother's female relatives, had not been, why
then did her mother express such worry about her, such disapproval, though reluctant to bring up the subject again, having once
murmured, "If you love each other, I don't see why . . ." meaning
I don't see why you don't get married, her voice trailing off into a
painful silence, for there was no reply, only a stiffening of her
daughter's shoulders, an angry hurt glistening in the eyes, and so,
now, running, hearing the wind high in the trees, or was it voices,
faint laughter, she told herself defiantly that she was not really
certain, not really, that she loved him, this man with whom she
lived who was not her husband, apart from the hunger that bound
her to him she did not know if she loved him, or could love any
man, though knowing that, however much she did, or did not, love
him, his feeling for her was less intense than hers for him, less
desperate, less hungry, and this was a fact about which she did not
care to think, for it pained her, it was a hurt lodged deep in her, and
in any case this was not the time for such thoughts, the happiness
of this moment, flying weightless and bodiless and nameless along
the trail that had now grown weedy thinking, *How different everything is, by day*, meaning *How different I am, by day*, she was a

strong woman, really, buoyed by joy and defiance in equal measure, running now along what appeared to be a parkland access road into which the hiking trail had invisibly merged, Lake Mt. Moriah behind her and to the left, this road with a look of being abandoned, densely bordered by deciduous trees, many of them birches, striking clumps of birches with thick, sturdy, white-glaring trunks very different from the smaller birches downstate, she saw that some of their leaves had turned prematurely, yellow, wizened, the symptoms, she'd read in an Adirondack publication, of stress caused by acid rain, pollution out of Chicago and its industrial environs blown eastward to fall as poisonous rain in the Adirondack wilderness, she wanted to cry with rage, she was furious, she was deeply wounded, one day soon she would break off her relationship with the man who was not her husband precisely because he was not her husband and he did not sense her need for him, her terrible hunger, how it demeaned her, when they returned to the city, perhaps, she was an independent woman, she was an ambitious woman, yes, she was willing to move to another part of the country and she was willing to move alone—*You don't love me as much as I love you, and so I hate you*—but of course she did not hate him, she loved him very much, unless that was simply her weakness, that love, of which, to him, she could never speak, and thinking of these things, vexed, disturbed, thinking of the very things she forbade herself to think of at this sacred time, this running time, this time of namelessness and flight and happiness, she drew the back of one hand across her forehead to wipe away the sweat, her scarf was damp, she heard laughter ringing on all sides, blinking to get her vision clear, she saw, ahead, several figures by the side of the road, young men they appeared to be, in their mid- or late twenties, campers, perhaps, hikers, they were dressed in shorts, or swimming trunks, bare-chested, they were talking and laughing loudly together, and then, noticing her, they quieted at once, the high-pitched laughter of one fading as, turning, he squinted in her direction to see what his companions had sighted, she would remember the sudden silence, and how, instinctively, hardly conscious of what she did, she glanced about to see if there were other figures close by, female figures, but there did not appear to be, she felt a stab of apprehension, thinking, *But I can't turn back, I won't turn back,* trying not to meet the men's frank rude assessing gazes, for she was not the kind of woman who anticipates harm from strangers, not at such a time, in a place of such natural beauty—*Not here, not now*—so she continued running along the road, the sun pounding at her temples, rivulets of chill sweat running down her sides, she did not consider herself a sexually attractive woman and she was several years older than these young men and once they got a clear look at her they would lose interest in her, she believed, her small, wan face, her overlarge intense eyes, her sensitive skin that exaggerated any blemish, her narrow lips, small breasts, she told herself this even as, running toward them, required to pass within a few yards of them since the trail led inexorably that way and to pause, to turn, to veer off suddenly in any other direction would be to acknowledge, to the men and to herself, that there was something between her and them to be acknowledged, she saw that they were staring with an unmistakable excitement, conferring together, one of them, thick-bodied, squat, his bare torso covered in coarse black hair, had already stepped quickly out onto the road as if to block her way, how very quickly he'd moved, by instinct, perhaps, sheer masculine instinct, the predator's instinct, yet, still, tasting panic now, she continued to run forward—*I can't stop, how can I stop: I will not*—she saw that one of the men had a growth of pale red whiskers, another, grinning, had fleshy lips, the one blocking her way was misshapen somehow, was he—a blunt hairless bullet head growing out of his shoulders, no neck, fatty-muscular upper arms, rolls of pale flesh at his stomach, the waist of his swimming trunks low enough to show his navel, a navel thickly whorled in dark hair, she saw his eyes, hot, derisive, hungry, in terror she was telling them, *I am not my body, I am more than a woman's body,* seeing the expectancy and arousal in their eyes, the crude appetite, the elation, how like dogs' mouths their grinning mouths, the teeth inside their grins—*Don't touch me any of you: God damn you!*—her vision blurred with tears of fury and helplessness and resignation as she ran into harsh sunlight as into oblivion, and then, so unexpectedly, she would recall afterward so miraculously, when she was within approximately twenty feet of the fattish young man blocking her way she saw how the expressions on the men's faces shifted, their eyes moving quick-silver in their sockets, their bodies too altering, almost imper-ceptibly, but unmistakably, they'd sighted something or someone behind her, in that instant she understood that the man who was not her husband and who did not love her with quite the hunger with which she loved him must have run into view, he'd known which branch of the trail to take, to follow her, very likely he'd been watching her all along, and so everything was changed—*I'm safe—saved*—as if the very sun had been extinguished and had then returned and all so instantaneously not a molecule in all of nature would register its unthinkable absence, let alone its miraculous return, she was safe, she was loved, not on her own terms but on another's, and this would be the terms of her life, these were the terms of her life, her eyes welled with tears that, undeserving as she was, she *was* safe and there remained no sign anyone might inter-pret to suggest that she had ever, for even the space of a minute, not been safe, for perhaps she had imagined everything? she had exag-gerated the danger? for now the young men showed friendly faces, still watchful, but smiling, glancing from her to the man who ran behind her, judging, yes, this was a couple, the woman was under the protection of the man, yes, they understood, nothing required articulation, for instinct prevailed, instinct is all, the young man with the reddish beard lifted a hand in greeting, and the fattish young man blocking her way was no longer blocking her way, he stepped off the road, mock graciously, with a friendly smirk, even as, maintaining her speed, her face showing none of the emotion she felt, she too stepped off the road, on the other side, running in the grass to avoid him, courtesy in her gesture as well as caution, and then she'd passed him and the others and saw ahead only the narrow road, the intermittent blaze of goldenrod, the dense border of trees, and the sky a high remote blue marbled with cloud, that thin tracery of white that scarcely moves, like a frieze, and behind her she heard men exchange greetings, the man who was not her husband and the young men by the road, the ritual of murmured greetings common to joggers, hikers, bicyclists of our time—''H'lo! How's it going!''—and no replies expected, and so that was what happened. Except, what had happened?

Pain

When you are in pain the pain is in you for the pain is you.

When you are in pain the pain is in you for the pain fits fully, like a hand thrust into a pliant glove. When you are in pain the pain is you and no one remains. When you are in pain you cannot be apprehensive of the future or regretful of the past for the pain is all present tense and the pain is you when you are in pain.

When you are in pain the pain is you and you have no need to name the pain or consider its causes, nor do you need to speak of future humiliations or hopes of happiness for the pain is you and you are utterly absorbed. When you are in pain you may be childish in weeping or stoic in character but you need not fear injury, malaise, long humid August days that ravel out to nothing, the despoiling of your name. When you are in pain you cannot be snubbed or unfairly judged since there is no one except the pain when you are in pain and the pain is you.

When you are not in immediate pain your body is alert and tense as a network of wires strung tight awaiting the return of pain for the pain will return for the pain is you. Such questions as *Will it flash? sting? pulse? pry? stab? hammer? throb? ripple? pierce? flood?* are inevitable questions when you are not in pain for you must antici-

pate pain for it has proven itself worthy. When you are not in pain
you are obliged to inhabit certain human postures as *pride, courage,*
calm, lucidity, Olympian detachment, patience, resiliency, "great
sense of humor," sweetness, charm, dignity, noblesse oblige, innate
good sense, common sense, rationality, optimism—and the rest.
When you are not in pain.

When you are not in pain you may be brave or cowardly as you
wish, for the pain awaits its terrible return and passes no judgment.
When you are not in pain you may "wallow in self-pity" (as they
say) or you may "deny" (as they say) by absorbing yourself in other
subjects. For the pain offers no opinion, presents no bias. When you
are not in pain you may hide your ghastly ravaged face behind your
hands or beg that all mirrors be taken from your sight or would you
wish all mirrors everywhere smashed? You may whisper gentle
reasonable requests that issue forth as screams. You may scream
until your vocal cords are raw but issue no sound. You may ring the
tiny golden bells at your bedside shyly or furiously as you wish. You
may brood over this packet of yellowed, creased old snapshots. You
may write desperate little notes to those whom you once loved and
betrayed and forgot. You may "contemplate" (as they say) suicide.
You may press your fevered face against the windowpane and when
no one sees you may despoil the exquisite frost filigrees with your
vile scum-coated tongue. For the pain is merely absent, and awaits
its return.

When you are in pain the pain is in you and in the space you inhabit
which is the room or the world or all you recall of either. When you
are in pain you have nothing to fear of vanity or sin or oversubtlety
or hyperesthesia or hypocrisy. When you are in pain and the pain
is in you you are without language and no one can pursue you into
that country for you are the pain and no one remains and even the
curvature of the earth and the slow dreamlike floating fall of the
moon through the sky and the myriad constellations of the great
sky have disappeared. When you are in pain the mirror's lead backing has dissolved so, for once, you must gaze into nothing. When
you are in pain and the pain is in you a sudden sweetness floods

your veins which is piercing sunshine on frost or dizzying arabesques in that wallpaper beside your head. When you are in pain and the pain is in you and the pain is you you can no more resist than a diver can resist gravity once he is falling through the air for there is no one to resist when you are in pain and the pain is in you and the pain is you. When the pain is.

Where *Is* Here?

For years they had lived without incident in their house in a quiet residential neighborhood when, one November evening at dusk, the doorbell rang, and the father went to answer it, and there on his doorstep stood a man he had never seen before. The stranger apologized for disturbing him at what was probably the dinner hour and explained that he'd once lived in the house—"I mean, I was a child in this house"—and since he was in the city on business he thought he would drop by. He had not seen the house since January 1949 when he'd been eleven years old and his widowed mother had sold it and moved away but, he said, he thought of it often, dreamt of it often, and never more powerfully than in recent months. The father said, "Would you like to come inside for a few minutes and look around?" The stranger hesitated, then said firmly, "I think I'll just poke around outside for a while, if you don't mind. That might be sufficient." He was in his late forties, the father's approximate age. He wore a dark suit, conservatively cut; he was hatless, with thin silver-tipped neatly combed hair; a plain, sober, intelligent face and frowning eyes. The father, reserved by nature, but genial and even gregarious when taken unaware, said amiably, "Of course we don't mind. But I'm afraid many things have changed since 1949."

So, in the chill, damp, deepening dusk, the stranger wandered around the property while the mother set the dining room table and the father peered covertly out the window. The children were upstairs in their rooms. "Where is he now?" the mother asked. "He just went into the garage," the father said. "The garage! What does he want in there!" the mother said uneasily. "Maybe you'd better go out there with him." "He wouldn't want anyone with him," the father said. He moved stealthily to another window, peering through the curtains. A moment passed in silence. The mother, paused in the act of setting down plates, neatly folded paper napkins, and stainless-steel cutlery, said impatiently, "And where is he now? I don't like this." The father said, "Now he's coming out of the garage," and stepped back hastily from the window. "Is he going now?" the mother asked. "I wish I'd answered the door." The father watched for a moment in silence then said, "He's headed into the backyard." "Doing what?" the mother asked. "Not *doing* anything, just walking," the father said. "He seems to have a slight limp." "Is he an older man?" the mother asked. "I didn't notice," the father confessed. "Isn't that just like you!" the mother said.

She went on worriedly, "He could be anyone, after all. Any kind of thief, or mentally disturbed person, or even murderer. Ringing our doorbell like that with no warning and you don't even know what he looks like!"

The father had moved to another window and stood quietly watching, his cheek pressed against the glass. "He's gone down to the old swings. I hope he won't sit in one of them, for memory's sake, and try to swing—the posts are rotted almost through." The mother drew breath to speak but sighed instead, as if a powerful current of feeling had surged through her. The father was saying, "Is it possible he remembers those swings from his childhood? I can't believe they're actually that old." The mother said vaguely, "They were old when we bought the house." The father said, "But we're talking about forty years or more, and that's a long time. The mother sighed again, involuntarily. "Poor man!" she murmured. She was standing before her table but no longer seeing it. In her hand were objects—forks, knives, spoons—she could not have named. She said, "We can't bar the door against him. That would be cruel." The father said, "What? No one has barred any door against anyone." "Put yourself in his place," the mother said. "He told me he didn't *want* to come inside," the father said. "Oh—isn't that just like you!'' the mother said in exasperation.

Without a further word she went to the back door and called out for the stranger to come inside, if he wanted, when he had finished looking around outside.

They introduced themselves rather shyly, giving names, and forgetting names, in the confusion of the moment. The stranger's handshake was cool and damp and tentative. He was smiling hard, blinking moisture from his eyes; it was clear that entering his childhood home was enormously exciting yet intimidating to him. Repeatedly he said, ''It's so nice of you to invite me in—I truly hate to disturb you—I'm really so grateful, and so—'' But the perfect word eluded him. As he spoke his eyes darted about the kitchen almost like eyes out of control. He stood in an odd stiff posture, hands gripping the lapels of his suit as if he meant to crush them. The mother, meaning to break the awkward silence, spoke warmly of their satisfaction with the house and with the neighborhood, and the father concurred, but the stranger listened only politely, and continued to stare, and stare hard. Finally he said that the kitchen had been so changed—''so modernized''—he almost didn't recognize it. The floor tile, the size of the windows, something about the position of the cupboards—all were different. But the sink was in the same place, of course; and the refrigerator and stove; and the door leading down to the basement—''That *is* the door leading down to the basement, isn't it?'' He spoke strangely, staring at the door. For a moment it appeared he might ask to be shown the basement but the moment passed, fortunately—this was not a part of their house the father and mother would have been comfortable showing to a stranger.

Finally, making an effort to smile, the stranger said, ''Your kitchen is so—pleasant.'' He paused. For a moment it seemed he had nothing further to say. Then, ''A—controlled sort of place. My mother— When we lived here—'' His words trailed off into a dreamy silence and the mother and father glanced at each other with carefully neutral expressions.

On the windowsill above the sink were several lushly blooming African violet plants in ceramic pots and these the stranger made a

show of admiring. Impulsively he leaned over to sniff the flowers—
"Lovely!"—though African violets have no smell. As if
embarrassed he said, "Mother too had plants on this windowsill but
I don't recall them ever blooming."

The mother said tactfully, "Oh they were probably the kind that
don't bloom—like ivy."

In the next room, the dining room, the stranger appeared to be
even more deeply moved. For some time he stood staring, wordless. With fastidious slowness he turned on his heel, blinking, and
frowning, and tugging at his lower lip in a rough gesture that
must have hurt. Finally, as if remembering the presence of his
hosts, and the necessity for some display of civility, the stranger
expressed his admiration for the attractiveness of the room, and
its coziness. He'd remembered it as cavernous, with a ceiling
twice as high. "And dark most of the time," he said wonderingly.
"Dark by day, dark by night." The mother turned the lights of
the little brass chandelier to their fullest: shadows were dispersed
like ragged ghosts and the cut-glass fruit bowl at the center of the
table glowed like an exquisite multifaceted jewel. The stranger
exclaimed in surprise. He'd extracted a handkerchief from his
pocket and was dabbing carefully at his face, where beads of perspiration shone. He said, as if thinking aloud, still wonderingly,
"My father was a unique man. Everyone who knew him admired
him. He sat *here*," he said, gingerly touching the chair that was in
fact the father's chair, at one end of the table. "And Mother sat
there," he said, merely pointing. "I don't recall my own place or
my sister's but I suppose it doesn't matter. . . . I see you have four
place settings, Mrs. . . . ? Two children, I suppose?" "A boy
eleven, and a girl thirteen," the mother said. The stranger stared
not at her but at the table, smiling. "And so too *we* were—I
mean, there were two of us: my sister and me."

The mother said, as if not knowing what else to say, "Are you—
close?"

The stranger shrugged, distractedly rather than rudely, and
moved on to the living room.

This room, cozily lit as well, was the most carefully furnished
room in the house. Deep-piled wall-to-wall carpeting in hunter

green, cheerful chintz drapes, a sofa and matching chairs in nubby
heather green, framed reproductions of classic works of art, a gleaming gilt-framed mirror over the fireplace: wasn't the living room
impressive as a display in a furniture store? But the stranger said
nothing at first. Indeed, his eyes narrowed sharply as if he were
confronted with a disagreeable spectacle. He whispered, "Here too!
Here too!"

He went to the fireplace, walking, now, with a decided limp; he
drew his fingers with excruciating slowness along the mantel as if
testing its materiality. For some time he merely stood, and stared,
and listened. He tapped a section of wall with his knuckles—
"There used to be a large water stain here, like a shadow."

"Was there?" murmured the father out of politeness, and "Was
there!" murmured the mother. Of course, neither had ever seen a
water stain there.

Then, noticing the window seat, the stranger uttered a soft surprised cry, and went to sit in it. He appeared delighted: hugging
his knees like a child trying to make himself smaller. "This was
one of my happy places! At least when Father wasn't home. I'd
hide away here for hours, reading, daydreaming, staring out the
window! Sometimes Mother would join me, if she was in the
mood, and we'd plot together—oh, all sorts of fantastical things!"
The stranger remained sitting in the window seat for so long,
tears shining in his eyes, that the father and mother almost feared
he'd forgotten them. He was stroking the velvet fabric of the
cushioned seat, gropingly touching the leaded windowpanes.
Wordlessly, the father and mother exchanged a glance: who was
this man, and how could they tactfully get rid of him? The father
made a face signaling impatience and the mother shook her head
without seeming to move it. For they couldn't be rude to a guest
in their house.

The stranger was saying in a slow, dazed voice, "It all comes back
to me now. How could I have forgotten! Mother used to read to me,
and tell me stories, and ask me riddles I couldn't answer. 'What
creature walks on four legs in the morning, two legs at midday,
three legs in the evening?' 'What is round, and flat, measuring mere
inches in one direction, and infinity in the other?' 'Out of what does

our life arise? Out of what does our consciousness arise? Why are we here? Where *is* here?' "

The father and mother were perplexed by these strange words and hardly knew how to respond. The mother said uncertainly, "Our daughter used to like to sit there too, when she was younger. It *is* a lovely place." The father said with surprising passion, "I hate riddles—they're moronic some of the time and obscure the rest of the time." He spoke with such uncharacteristic rudeness, the mother looked at him in surprise.

Hurriedly she said, "Is your mother still living, Mr. . . . ?" "Oh no. Not at all," the stranger said, rising abruptly from the window seat, and looking at the mother as if she had said something mildly preposterous. "I'm sorry," the mother said. "Please don't be," the stranger said. "We've all been dead—*they've* all been dead—a long time."

The stranger's cheeks were deeply flushed as if with anger and his breath was quickened and audible.

The visit might have ended at this point but so clearly did the stranger expect to continue on upstairs, so purposefully, indeed almost defiantly, did he limp his way to the stairs, neither the father nor the mother knew how to dissuade him. It was as if a force of nature, benign at the outset, now uncontrollable, had swept its way into their house! The mother followed after him saying nervously, "I'm not sure what condition the rooms are in, upstairs. The children's rooms especially—" The stranger muttered that he did not care in the slightest about the condition of the household and continued on up without a backward glance.

The father, his face burning with resentment and his heart accelerating as if in preparation for combat, had no choice but to follow the stranger and the mother up the stairs. He was flexing and unflexing his fingers as if to rid them of stiffness.

On the landing, the stranger halted abruptly to examine a stained-glass fanlight—"My God, I haven't thought of this in years!" He spoke excitedly of how, on tiptoe, he used to stand and peek out through the diamonds of colored glass, red, blue, green, golden yellow: seeing with amazement the world outside so *altered*. "After such a lesson it's hard to take the world on its own terms, isn't it?" he asked. The father asked, annoyed, "On what terms should it be taken, then?" The stranger replied, regarding him levelly, with a just perceptible degree of disdain, "Why, none at all."

It was the son's room—by coincidence, the stranger's old room— the stranger most wanted to see. Other rooms on the second floor, the "master" bedroom in particular, he decidedly did not want to see. As he spoke of it, his mouth twitched as if he had been offered something repulsive to eat.

The mother hurried on ahead to warn the boy and to straighten up his room a bit. No one had expected a visitor this evening! "So you have two children," the stranger murmured, looking at the father with a small quizzical smile. "Why?" The father stared at him as if he hadn't heard correctly. " 'Why'?" he asked. "Yes. *Why?*" the stranger repeated. They looked at each other for a long strained moment, then the stranger said quickly, "But you love them—of course." The father controlled his temper and said, biting off his words, "Of course."

"Of course, of course," the stranger murmured, tugging at his necktie and loosening his collar, "otherwise it would all come to an end." The two men were of approximately the same height but the father was heavier in the shoulders and torso; his hair had thinned more severely so that the scalp of the crown was exposed, flushed, damp with perspiration, sullenly alight.

With a stiff avuncular formality the stranger shook the son's hand. "So this is your room, now! So you live here, now!" he murmured, as if the fact were an astonishment. Not used to shaking hands, the boy was stricken with shyness and cast his eyes down. The stranger limped past him, staring. "The same!—the same!—walls, ceiling, floor—window—" He drew his fingers slowly along the windowsill; around the frame; rapped the glass, as if, again, testing materiality; stooped to look outside—but it was night, and nothing but his reflection bobbed in the glass, ghostly and insubstantial. He groped against the walls, he opened the closet door before the mother could protest, he sat heavily on the boy's bed, the springs creaking beneath him. He was panting, red-faced, dazed. "And the ceiling overhead," he whispered. He nodded slowly and repeatedly, smiling. "And the floor beneath. That is what *is*."

He took out his handkerchief again and fastidiously wiped his face. He made a visible effort to compose himself.

The father, in the doorway, cleared his throat and said, "I'm afraid it's getting late—it's almost six."

The mother said, "Oh yes I'm afraid—I'm afraid it *is* getting late. There's dinner, and the children have their homework—"

The stranger got to his feet. At his full height he stood for a precarious moment swaying, as if the blood had drained from his head and he was in danger of fainting. But he steadied himself with a hand against the slanted dormer ceiling. He said, "Oh yes!—I know!—I've disturbed you terribly!—you've been so *kind.*" It seemed, surely, as if the stranger *must* leave now, but, as chance had it, he happened to spy, on the boy's desk, an opened mathematics textbook and several smudged sheets of paper, and impulsively offered to show the boy a mathematical riddle—"You can take it to school tomorrow and surprise your teacher!"

So, out of dutiful politeness, the son sat down at his desk and the stranger leaned familiarly over him, demonstrating adroitly with a ruler and a pencil how "what we call 'infinity' " can be contained within a small geometrical figure on a sheet of paper. "First you draw a square; then you draw a triangle to fit inside the square; then you draw a second triangle, and a third, and a fourth, each to fit inside the square, but without their points coinciding, and as you continue—here, son, I'll show you—give me your hand, and I'll show you—the border of the triangles' common outline gets more complex and measures larger, and larger, and larger—and soon you'll need a magnifying glass to see the details, and then you'll need a microscope, and so on and so forth, forever, laying triangles neatly down to fit inside the original square *without their points coinciding*—!" The stranger spoke with increasing fervor; spittle gleamed in the corners of his mouth. The son stared at the geometrical shapes rapidly materializing on the sheet of paper before him with no seeming comprehension but with a rapt staring fascination as if he dared not look away.

After several minutes of this the father came abruptly forward and dropped his hand on the stranger's shoulder. "The visit is over,'' he said calmly. It was the first time since they'd shaken hands that the two men had touched, and the touch had a galvanic effect upon the stranger: he dropped ruler and pencil at once, froze in his stooped posture, burst into frightened tears.

Now the visit truly was over; the stranger, at last, *was* leaving, having wiped away his tears and made a stoical effort to compose himself; but on the doorstep, to the father's astonishment, he made a final, preposterous appeal—he wanted to see the basement. "Just to sit on the stairs? In the dark? For a few quiet minutes? And you could close the door and forget me, you and your family could have your dinner and—"

The stranger was begging but the father was resolute. Without raising his voice he said, "No. *The visit is over.*"

He shut the door, and locked it.

Locked it! His hands were shaking and his heart beat angrily.

He watched the stranger walk away—out to the sidewalk, out to the street, disappearing in the darkness. Had the streetlights gone out?

Behind the father the mother stood apologetic and defensive, wringing her hands in a classic stance. "Wasn't that sad! Wasn't that—*sad!* But we had no choice but to let him in, it was the only decent thing to do." The father pushed past her without comment. In the living room he saw that the lights were flickering as if on the brink of going out; the patterned wallpaper seemed drained of color; a shadow lay upon it shaped like a bulbous cloud or growth. Even the robust green of the carpeting looked faded. Or was it an optical illusion? Everywhere the father looked, a pulse beat mute with rage. "*I* wasn't the one who opened the door to that man in the first place," the mother said, coming up behind the father and touching his arm. Without seeming to know what he did the father violently jerked his arm and thrust her away.

"Shut up. We'll forget it," he said.

"But—"

"*We'll forget it.*"

The mother entered the kitchen walking slowly as if she'd been struck a blow. In fact, a bruise the size of a pear would materialize on her forearm by morning. When she reached out to steady herself she misjudged the distance of the door frame—or did the doorframe recede an inch or two—and nearly lost her balance.

In the kitchen the lights were dim and an odor of sourish smoke, subtle but unmistakable, made her nostrils pinch.

She slammed open the oven door. Grabbed a pair of pot holders with insulated linings. "*I* wasn't the one, God damn you," she cried, panting, "and you know it."